Cold Truth

RICHARD WOODMAN

First published in 2020 by Sharpe Books.

Contents

THE ADELPHI HOTEL, LIVERPOOL, MARCH 1943
THE FIRST EVENING - DADDY'S YACHT
THE SECOND EVENING - THE SHIP OF FOOLS
THE THIRD EVENING - THE WHITE ISLAND
THE FOURTH EVENING - THE SECRET
LONDON, MAY 1945.
AUTHOR'S NOTE

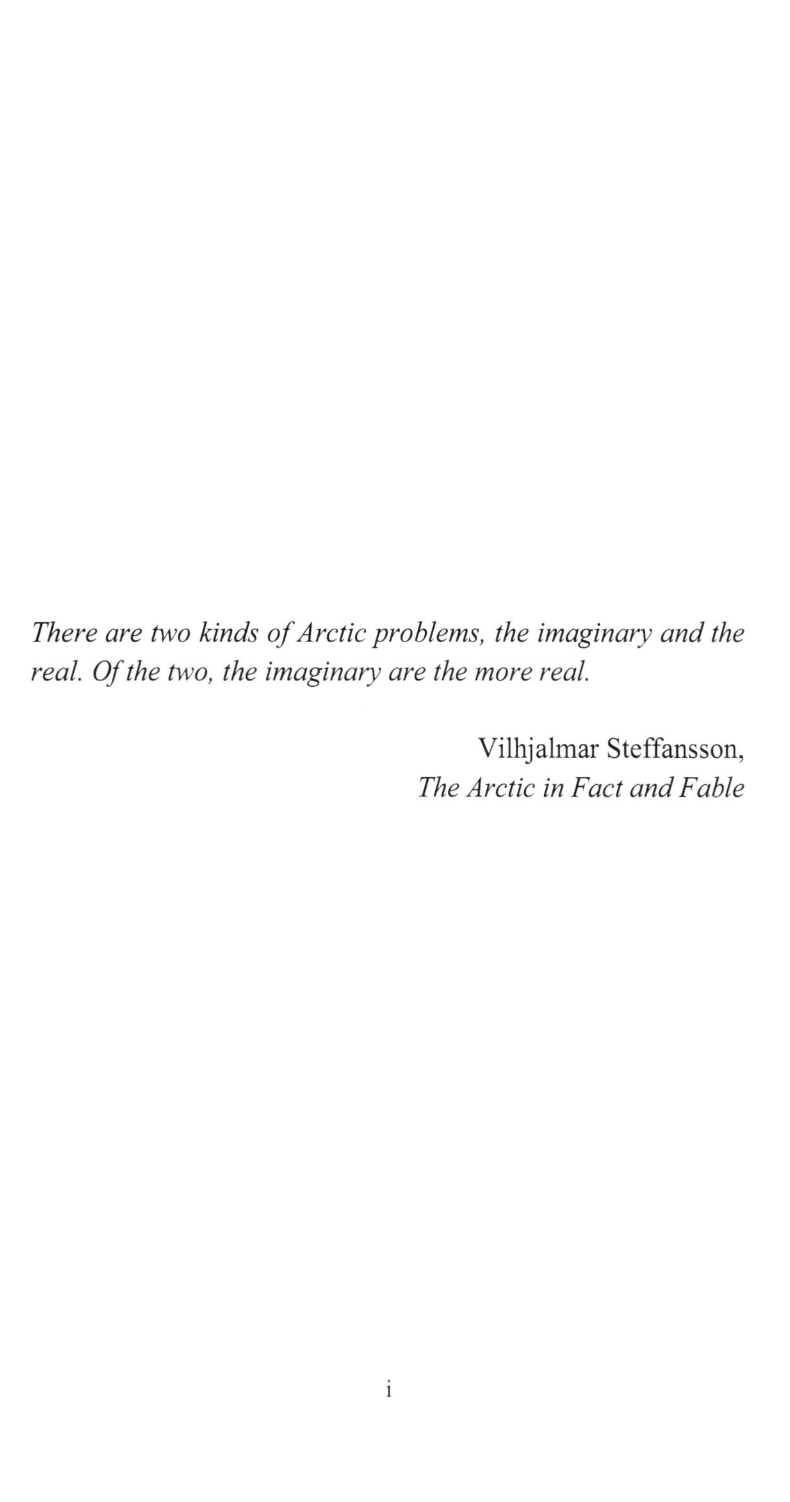

There are two kinds of Arctic problems, the imaginary and the real. Of the two, the imaginary are the more real.

Vilhjalmar Steffansson,
The Arctic in Fact and Fable

She knew she had found him the instant her eyes adjusted to the light inside the Adelphi Hotel and she could see through the clouds of tobacco smoke that whorled in the thick, hot and heavy air. He was sitting quite alone at the far end of the bar itself.

' "Call me Ishmael," ' she quoted to herself with a small sense of triumph.

The chill of the night outside and the depressing darkness of the blackout were banished in the main bar. Here the cares of the war had been set aside in favour of a brittle, desperate gaiety which presaged little happiness – howsoever brief – but a good deal of hang-overs, or worse, the following morning.

She wove her way between the tables, resisting the odd attempt to catch her attention made by the young men lounging in their chairs, most of them wearing the uniform of junior or middle-ranking officers of the two naval reserves, and ignoring the glares from the women who regarded her with deep suspicion and her presence upon their 'patch' as a presumption. Only the waiters seemed to afford her the degree of courtesy she might have expected; all of them were old men, beyond the age for military service and the clutches of the state.

He was staring at the long mirror behind the rows of bottles and their optics, objects that were pretty much the only sign of plenty in Liverpool in March 1943. A first glance suggested a misanthropic alcoholic, but as she drew closer she thought there was rather more to him than that. She knew what he looked like, or rather what he *had* looked like fifteen or so years earlier when he had worked for her father, for she had seen the photographs in her father's portfolio. It was only to be expected that he had lost the boyish exuberance that shone through the group picture of the ship's crew; she knew enough of the trials of the Battle of the Atlantic to know that, notwithstanding the excoriating experiences of the young men raising the raucous hubbub in the Adelphi bar that evening, fifteen years had wrought its own ineluctable transformation. Had either factor reduced him to a misanthropic alcoholic she would not have condemned him, for among the years in question the world had been subjected to the Great Depression and - more recently, she happened to know - the losses of shipping in the North Atlantic convoys had reached a terrifying level.

As she covered the few yards between the door to the bar-room and the far end of the bar itself, she thought he appeared remarkably detached, and not merely from the fact that he sat alone, with several vacant bar-stools between him and the next drinker. There was no sense that he waiting for anyone, or that he was swallowing the pink gin in front of him with immoderate speed. Indeed, of all the men in that noisy, smoky, over-blown chamber, he seemed entirely self-contained and self-absorbed, and she knew she was going to be breaking into his train of thought. She quailed somewhat at the prospect, an odd sensation for one of her own experience and profession and she seemed borne up alongside him on a wave of enthusiasm that would shortly find itself dragged back into the general mayhem of the bar like a wavelet drawn back into the greater ocean by the undertow upon a beach.

'Good evening, Commander,' she said as she reached his side in a breathless voice that hoped to make its mark.

'*Lieutenant* Commander,' he responded without turning his head, so that she felt the effect of intrusion more keenly than ever.

'I thought it was naval protocol to...' He broke into her explanation.

'I'm not interested,' he said curtly, still staring ahead, and the presumption that she was a prostitute touting for business stung her. Suddenly the imminence of the undertow vanished and her professional persistence kicked-in.

'You don't know why I approached you,' she protested.

'Don't I?' He turned towards her, adding, 'you're a bloody reporter and you should know better: "careless talk costs lives",' he quoted, nodding at the poster on the wall beyond the end of the bar. It showed a glamorous vamp reclining on a chair surrounded by a bevy of red-faced and obviously inebriated army, naval and air-force officers all bragging about their exploits. She was genuinely surprised and kicked herself when she realised that, far from not looking at her, he had been observing her rather obvious progress across the bar-room in the mirror.

'What is it you want?'

His tone was curt, dismissive and distinctly unfriendly. She flicked a quick look at herself in the mirror as if to reassure herself that she had not changed, a touch of female vanity that at least told her she was not unattractive. The quick glance did not go unobserved.

'You remind me of my wife,' he added abruptly, picking a silver cigarette case off a book that she had not noticed lay on the bar in front of him. He opened it, took out a cigarette, put it in his mouth and lit it with a lighter that lay beside the book. The snub in not offering one to her was obvious. 'As I said, I am not interested.' As he spoke the cigarette bobbed up and down between his lips and the lighter flame danced under his breath.

'Interested enough to compare me to your wife,' she interjected quickly, sliding onto the adjacent vacant bar-stool. 'Did she give you the cigarette case?'

He cast his eyes down at the silver box and, involuntarily she thought, his fingers touched it, before he turned towards her and blew smoke directly into her face.

'Fuck off,' he said quietly, finishing the pink gin, pocketing the cigarette case and the lighter, picking up his book and sliding off the bar stool. Ignoring the obscenity, she noticed how tall he was, tall and rangy; that he had not lost from that long-ago photograph.

'I'm sorry if I offended you,' she said hurriedly, laying her hand on the two and a half rings of inter-twined gold lace on his sleeve in an attempt not to lose her quarry, 'but how did you know I was a reporter?'

'I said, fuck off. That ought to be clear to a woman of even your apparent insensibility…'

'That's fucking misogynistic of you!' she snapped back so sharply that he checked his departure. His mouth, which she thought for a moment would smile at the riposte, suddenly hardened and his eyes flashed something worse, something that she could not define but did not like.

He arrested his dismissive departure and his eyes narrowed, focussing on her with a disturbing intensity. 'You *do* have an uncanny and disturbing likeness to my wife,' he said with a sudden intensity, 'so-much-so that for a moment, just one happy bloody moment, I thought you were her - back from the dead.' He straightened up from this obtrusive and rude scrutiny. 'There is no misogyny in personal grief, young lady.' He paused, then went on, indicating the racket around them: 'All this crapulous nonsense is to be endured, like the war itself, until we either die or get the opportunity to rebuild our broken lives – those of us that have had our lives broken that is. You, I surmise, are rather enjoying it all…' He ground out his cigarette end in the ashtray.

She flushed at that.

'I rather thought so.' He sighed and then surprised her by resuming his seat on the bar-stool. 'What would you like to drink?'

She was fiddling in her hand-bag and he thought she was either about to cry or get her note-book out; instead she produced a packet of cigarettes, opened it and, without a word, offered him one.

'*Touché*,' he said with a smile. 'No, thanks. Now tell me what you want with me and what you want to drink.'

'I'll have a vermouth, thank you, but first tell me how you knew me for a reporter?'

'Oh, I don't know, it's written all over you…' she was about to protest that that was nonsense when he added with another sigh, 'no, when I realised that you weren't a reincarnation of Moira, I realised who you are. You see Moira was not infrequently taken for your elder sister.'

'Oh!' was all she could manage.

He was laughing now. 'You *are* Lord Southmoore's daughter, aren't you?' She nodded. 'And you were at the launching of the S.S. *Clytemnestra* as a small girl…'

'I was seven!' she protested.

Yes, well, since then you have grown up, but I was actually introduced to your father as one of the ship's apprentices, he and Richard Holt, one of the owners, were great chums. So - your turn - why have you importuned me here tonight?'

'That's a very Shakespearean turn of phrase,' she said, relaxing as she sipped the vermouth he had ordered, and dragging the cigarette smoke down into her lungs.

'Oh God, just when I was beginning to get over my prejudice against you, you appear to have imbibed that national notion that merchant seamen in general and especially merchant mates turned naval officer, are ignorant buggers who have got out of their proper station in life because of this war. I sometimes wish it were true. You should go and write an article about the unsung heroes of the Western Approaches who keep this God-forsaken country in the fight against Hitler and forget about the Brylcream Boys in their Spitfires… Sorry, I'm having a rant…'

'But it was a very bad convoy and you emerged at the end of

it with a commendation for a DSC…'

'What in God's name are you talking about? They don't throw Distinguished Service Crosses around after the debacle to which…' he checked himself abruptly, biting his lip with anger at his failure to take his own advice.

For a moment she thought he was about to relapse into his former mood and quickly said, 'Your corvette, the *Nemesia*, is in dock, boiler cleaning; you have five day's grace, having sent your young officers off on leave…'

'Christ! Have you been round to see Uncle Max in Derby House? Or is this all privileged information known only unto the daughter of Lord Southmoore?'

'You met my father again,' she said, ignoring the remark and stubbing her own cigarette out (he noticed the red lipstick on its filter tip and that she had barely smoked it), 'some time after Richard Holt presented you to him at the launching of that dreadfully named ship, and no, I have not been round to see Admiral Horton, nor entered the portals of the place you mentioned, though he knows I am in Liverpool.'

'All the privileges of being not merely a red-hot reporter but the actual daughter of the newspaper baron that owns your rag, eh?' he said sardonically, aware that he had been injudicious in his choice of words.

'That's right,' she replied coolly. 'Daddy got me a job as a War Correspondent on the Home Front…'

'Then what on earth are you doing *importuning* a poor, half-cut, half-naval officer in this ante-room to hell, eh?'

'Because I didn't come here to talk about the war, or your part in it…'

'Go on… Is this about my second meeting with your rich daddy?'

'Yes.'

'Ahh.'

‘He has privileged access…’

‘I’m sure he has!’

‘Stop being so bloody rude and I’ll answer your question,’ she snapped. ‘You can give me one of your cigarettes by way of reparation.’

‘Can I?’ he said archly fishing the silver case from his pocket and ordering two more drinks.

She touched his hand with hers to steady it as he flicked on the lighter as she leaned forward. ‘How did your wife die?’ she asked quietly as he pocketed the lighter and she removed the cigarette from her lips.

He gave her a level stare and said in a flat voice devoid of any emotion, ‘she was visiting an old school friend in Hendon when one of ours came over and attempted to ditch an over heavy bomb-load in the Welsh Harp. Poor bastard dropped it short and it devastated a large number of houses. She was dragged out, or what was left of her was dragged out of the rubble by a Special Constable. Ironic, eh? Wrong place, wrong time and she gets killed by a…’

‘A Handley Page bomber from Hatfield…’

‘Yes; something like that. You obviously known all about it; they wouldn’t tell us a bloody thing, though everyone seemed to know it was a cock-up.’ He stopped speaking and she saw his jaw muscles working.

‘No wonder you don’t like the Brylcream boys.’

He turned back towards her. ‘What? Oh, oh no, it’s not due to that. Anyway, that’s all history now.’ He smiled wanly. ‘Thank God for small mercies; we had no children, though she was expecting… Such a bloody pity…’ He coughed, aware that she had got his guard down. ‘But none of this has got anything to do with this, er, interview, so…’ He gestured to her to go on.

‘Daddy… my father got wind of your commendation for sinking a U-boat. Not many people have done that.’

'Oh, it's unconfirmed,' he said dismissively. 'Anyone can release a bucket full of galley scraps…'

'You know that's not true…'

'I don't know anything. It's a feature of serving His Majesty in the Western Approaches.'

'Well, the point is my father recognised your name and recalled your earlier association…'

'*Association*, eh?' he said drily, raising one eyebrow.

'Will you please stop interrupting me!'

'I'm sorry; go on.'

'Well, he wants the whole story of the voyage he financed to the Arctic…'

'Oh, no! He has all the reports he needed…'

'You're interrupting again. You found them didn't you? And you concealed the information from my father who spent over one hundred thousand pounds on what could have been a remarkable scoop…'

'Is that how he saw it? A bad investment? Well, I'm sorry about that, but money isn't everything, you know – though perhaps you don't. Anyway, he could afford it. I should think sales of *The Courier…*'

She ignored the snide dig and persisted in her quest. 'You are the last of the officers alive…'

'No I'm not. Nat Gardner…' he stopped, reading the expression in her eyes. 'Oh, Christ, no.'

'When were you last in touch with him?'

'We saw each other in Singapore, no Hong Kong, not long before the outbreak of the war. We exchanged letters a couple of times after that and…don't tell me he is dead…'

'In a lifeboat in the South Atlantic… He was injured abandoning ship, I believe.'

'He must have been,' he said softly. 'Nat would have relished a challenge like an open-boat voyage, bless him.'

His affection touched her as a silence fell between them, broken at last when he sighed, ordered another round and said in a firmer voice, 'that's a damned shame. He was among the best, the very, very best.' After a further pause he rallied to ask: 'So, what does Daddy want now that he has sent you hot-foot here to Liverpool at a time he knows some of us have other things on our minds? Some form of indemnity for his wasted one hundred thousand? He got a few photographs and a good deal of kudos for his philanthropy, at least at the beginning. It was international philanthropy at that, for it was not at all a jingoistic expedition. No beefing up the jolly old British Empire; I admired him for that. I'd have thought to a chap with everything that would have been consolation enough, or has this got something to do with Madame Blavatskoya and her communications with "the other side"? God knows a lot of poor devils who lost people in the last bloody war were misled by Madame Blavatskoya and her ilk. If anyone should be harried for compensation it is that perpetrating bitch…'

'You're ranting again.'

'Maybe I am,' he said shortly and then, recalling something else he asked. 'Anyway, the whole world found out the answer to the question not long after we came back. Those Norwegian sealers found them all….'

'That's not the point. My father knows the voyage he financed found something and that it was not reported to him as it should have been. Moreover, Madame Blavatskoya was right, wasn't she? They *were* on the White Island. That information alone would have assuaged him. He did not share your contempt for Blavatskoya and her ilk, not least because he lost his own brother and his eldest son, my brother, on the Western front…'

'I'm sorry,' he said, looking, she thought, rather sweet in his mood of genuine apology.

'Anyway, Daddy was never offered a proper explanation as

to what exactly happened on the voyage, not even by the doctor whom he had sent along…

‘Oh, yes, old Crichton…’ his face darkened. ‘I remember him very well.’

‘He died on the expedition which, I believe ended in a bit of a shambles…’

‘It most certainly did,’ he snapped, the harsh tone back in his voice. He was going to say more, but bit his lip, allowing her to go on.

Well, my father knew several things had gone wrong and although the story was spun in the way indicated in the survivors’ reports I think he wants to know all about it now because he is not well and it is troubling him deeply. It has nothing to do with the money.’

‘He’s dying?’

‘Yes.’

‘I’m sorry,’ he said again, softly now. With a suddenly and unexpected tenderness he reached out and touched her hand. ‘I am truly sorry. I actually rather liked him.’

‘Well,’ she said stoically, ‘there’s a war on and there’s a lot of it about. Death, I mean. He’s an old man and…well, there it is.’ He remained silent as she recovered herself. ‘The problem is he has always had a great desire to get to the bottom of things. It is what made him a newspaperman in the first place.’

He nodded and smiled. ‘Of course. And there is the hundred thousand. I suppose that I’d feel the same. Tell me, did he try and find out from Gardner?’

‘Yes. They were in touch. I’m not certain how Daddy located him but he refused to say anything. His excuse was that you were the senior man and he would do nothing either without your approval, or in your stead.’

He smiled. ‘Nathaniel would say that, God rest his soul. But what happened to Alan Tomkins?’

'Who?'

'The *Alert*'s Chief Officer.'

She frowned. 'Oh, I don't know, he was untraceable.'

'That's a shame. He was a splendid fellow in his very distinct and undervalued way. So I am your last hope, or at least your father's?'

She nodded. 'Please humour him.'

'So what do you want me to do, come down to London on my next long leave and spill the beans?'

'No. Neither of you may live that long… I'm sorry to be so frank…'

He patted her hand again and offered her the lop-sided grin. 'No, you're right, in my case most certainly. Well what then?'

'You have a five-day boiler-clean…'

'Four after tonight…'

'Will you stop bloody interrupting me, Commander! I buy you dinner here, each night and you – as you put it – spill the beans. Will you do it?'

He blew out his cheeks and looked at her for some moments. 'Yes,' he said at last, patting her hand again. 'Yes, of course I will. War changes everything.'

'Thank you so much…'

'By the way, what is your name?'

'Call me Liz, or Lizzie. Until tomorrow then. Here at six.' She slipped from the bar stool, kissed him lightly on the cheek and was gone.

He stared after her in the mirror for a moment, then pushed aside the half-finished pink gin, picked up his book and left for his bed-room on an upper floor of the labyrinthine building that had become part naval ward-room, part knocking-shop.

THE FIRST EVENING - DADDY'S YACHT

I have to confess I found your father's expedition vessel unimpressive when I first saw her. She lay in a corner of the Surrey Commercial Dock on the Thames, sharing that filthy expanse of water with a handful of the usual undistinguished middle-trade vessels and a brace of coasters. One of these was leaving as I arrived in my taxi with my kit, a long quarter-decker belonging to Munro Brothers of Glasgow and I watched her for a moment after I had paid-off the cab and before I looked at the *Alert* properly. By contrast the coaster was vibrant with life, for there is nothing deader than a ship before her crew joins her and she remains in the hands of others, a ship-keeper, a gang of riggers. Besides, this was a wet and windy afternoon in late March, much the same time of year as this, which only added to the extreme bleakness of the moment. I wondered what I had let myself in for.

Despite her three masts, she seemed to be little more than an extension of the slime and slurry of the dock-side, much of which had been tramped up her gangway onto her wooden decks. I guessed, rightly as it transposed, that she was rigged as an auxiliary barque, a low-powered steamer with a simple sailing rig, though those yards that were then across her main and foremasts were a-cockbill and bereft of sails. Two, the main and fore topgallants, still lay across the deck, among an apparent tangle of extra-flexible steel wire rope and the ends of gantlines dangling from the fore and main-masts where the riggers had left them for the night when they knocked off.

Underneath her light dusting of London's finest soot there shot the odd gleam of recently applied paint, which told me she had but recently emerged from a graving dock and a glance at her topsides and waterline where her red boot-topping fought for attention with the unspeakable detritus that had accumulated between her hull and the dock-side. I noticed all this during the process of dragging my kit aboard: one trunk, a suitcase and a sextant box.

Altogether, she looked like an ex-sealer, being too small for a former whaler; a miniature version of Scott's *Discovery*, Bruce's *Scotia* or Shackleton's *Nimrod*, and she gave off the smell of a vessel employed in some such predatory trade. I thought with a wry smile of my father's enthusiasm for getting this appointment, so I had better explain how it all came about, because on the face of it, it was incongruous. Unlike many mercantile marine cadets and apprentices of my generation, I did not serve my indentures in sail; I was a steam man and proud of it, having been bound apprentice to Alfred Holt & Co. of Liverpool, owners of the *Clytemnestra*, the *Antigone* and about a hundred other fine vessels of similar Homeric nomenclature that made up the Blue Funnel Line.

They called us midshipmen too, just to inject us with the necessary sense of elitism to carry us through four years of rust chipping, painting, wire splicing and learning seamanship and navigation before casting us out into the wilderness. You couldn't hold officer's rank in the Blue Funnel Line without a master mariner's certificate. To obtain this required several years of sea-time and the acquisition of both a second mate's and a first mate's certificate of competency on the way, and you couldn't get this sea-time without going to sea in anything that floated. The objective was to get the sea-time in as soon as possible, so one's best option was to get one's second mate's ticket, then find a berth on a tramp ship. One could be away for a two-year voyage, by which time you could sit for first mate's, then do a second and qualify to sit for master. Things have changed a bit since then, thanks to Adolf and his gang of hooligans, but in those days the slump in world trade after the first war didn't help and I found myself kicking my heels at home with my parents in Surrey in the autumn of twenty-five, aged twenty-two and with less than fifty quid in the bank, money needed to sustain me during my next ticket leave, the big one, master's, with which I could rejoin Holt's.

My parents had never been keen on my going to sea; I was expected to qualify as a doctor, and follow my esteemed pater into a rather successful general practice, but I had neither the brains nor the application and had been too early seduced by a lot of romantic literature about the sea. I should like to have gone into sail, like most lads did, but my father procured me a place aboard the training-ship-cum-minor public school, HMS *Conway*, on the Mersey, where two strong influences came to work upon my future. Where I had failed at school, I found myself quite good aboard the *Conway*. I won a couple of prizes and came under the purview of Holt's, who put money into the old wooden wreck and regarded their *droits de seigneur* was to take the pick of the cadets as middies into their Blue Funnel liners. We also emerged as midshipmen in the Royal Naval Reserve, which is, I suppose, the kicking-off point by which I am, today, in command of that tin box of a corvette whose name you are quite illegally in possession of.

Anyway, there I was in the leafy hills of Surrey, chewing my intestines with anxiety, irritating my oh-so-successful father – 'diseases are not dependent upon world trade, my boy. They are a constant, like death and taxes, blah, blah,' a note of delicate protest from my mother at the other end of the breakfast table – and then he suddenly sat bolt upright.

'Good God!' He peered round the pages of the newspaper, *The Courier*, you'll be pleased to note and commanded us to listen before reading out loud: 'Navigating officers required for expedition to the Arctic, apply Box 24, *The Courier*, Fleet Street…' Then he collapsed the paper in his lap and stared pointedly at me. 'Well?'

I took the hint; a letter of application was in the late morning post and, two days later I was ushered into a waiting-room in *The Courier*'s Fleet Street head-quarters, which you know well. To be truthful it was not what I had expected, thinking only that *The Courier* was the vehicle by which the advertisement had been promulgated but it was obvious from the presence of eight other men, mostly young like myself, but some older and desperate, family men whose economic circumstances were increasingly dire as the world headed for the Wall Street Crash, that there was more going on than met the eye. Shortly after I sat down the tall figure of Nat Gardner entered the room. I noticed he had a rolled copy of *The Courier* under his arm. I could see its red-top thingamajig, you know the winged figure and then I realised that several other candidates also carried the bloody paper, and I chid myself for my stupidity in not purchasing a copy but, as a seaman, reading a daily newspaper was a luxury I had never acquired and I felt a wave of resentment that my father had not thought of it. Anyway, it was too late now. It was good to see Gardner. He was another Blue Flue middie and we knew each other, not well, but well enough to express genuine greetings and an exchange of commiseration at our collective circumstances.

'I won't have a snowball's hope in Hell,' he said in his booming voice, looking round the collection of mercantile marine hopefuls. 'What've you got, a first mate's?' I nodded, somewhat embarrassed at Nat's failure to understand the occasional necessity for *sotto voce* communications. 'I've only got second mate's…'

'And there are master mariners here,' a voice interjected with some asperity from a thin man sitting in the corner with a blue gabardine raincoat crushed in his lap. A moment later I was relieved from this tense atmosphere when a trim young lady,

Doris, as I learned later, your father's private secretary, called out my name. 'Mr Adams? Please follow me.'

I left the room with Nat's hissed 'Good luck' in my ears and followed the lovely Doris into a lift which whisked us up to your father's private office where I was offered a chair set in front of his desk.

Besides your father, one other man sat at the end of the desk. He was round faced, rather flushed about the gills with those unpleasant whiskers some men affect on their cheek-bones despite their being called 'bugger's grips'. Your father introduced himself and forbore from mentioning any previous contact.

'This is Commander Hanslip,' he added, and the red faced chap rose and extended his hand. So I first met Herbert Henry Hanslip, or "H.H.H" as he liked to be thought of in his more Shackeltonian moments. Unfortunately he was to prove no Shackleton, not even a pale shadow of the great man. The two of them quizzed me about my experience, Hanslip being obviously put-off by my lack of familiarity with sailing-ships and I left after about twenty minutes firmly convinced that I had no chance of the job. I did not pass through the waiting-room again, so had no chance to say anything to Nat Gardner and, as neither of us had the other's address, I presumed contact was lost, or at least dropped for the time being, a familiar occurrence to officers of the mercantile marine.

'How d'you get on?' my father asked over dinner that evening and I explained, with some heat, that if he hadn't sent me to *Conway* and I had served my time in sail I might have a job. He didn't understand, and I don't think he wanted to understand, the nuances that affect the career of merchant Jack. Anyway gloom descended upon the Adams' household and the following morning I began to write a letter to Their Lordships at the Admiralty in an attempt to find a posting in the Royal

Naval Reserve to which I had a tentative entrée thanks to my having been a midshipmite at *Conway*.

My heart wasn't really in it. Somehow that *voyage to the Arctic* had wormed its way under my skin and I was decidedly irritated to consider myself unqualified. Like all young men I was full of hope and optimism and took no thought about Hanslip, whose function I had not even considered, but I was stirred by the notion of going north, all my previous experience as a midshipman in the Blue Funnel Line being confined to the flying-fish trades of the Far East – give or take the odd typhoon – or the dull drudgery of tramping with coal or railway lines to India and carrying jute gunnies somewhere else between the two Tropics.

I was chewing the end of my fountain pen when I heard the door-bell ring and the maid's voice and then my mother's. The next thing I knew my mother called me and handed me a brown envelope with the remark that I had received a telegram.

It read: 'POSITION OF SECOND OFFICER OFFERED STOP IF INTERESTED REPORT THE COURIER TEN TOMORROW STOP SOUTHMOORE'.

I handed it to my mother and she smiled. 'That's wonderful,' she responded smiling. Adding typically, 'your father will be *so* pleased.'

When I was shown into *The Courier*'s waiting room a second time that week there were just three of us, the chief, second and third officers, appointed to the expedition. To my delight my junior was to be Nat Gardner while the man selected to be our chief mate was a complete stranger; I had not even noticed him at the interview but he rose and introduced himself as Alan Tomkins.

'I've a master's certificate in sail,' he said quietly. I recall having the impression there was a good deal more to Mr Tomkins that that enviable qualification, but perhaps I have misremembered. What I do recall with perfect clarity was that he was a powerfully built man of about forty, with deeply lined and weather-beaten features, severely scraped by the daily application of a razor, a thin mouth and incredibly blue eyes. A dusting of yellow hair was cut short and his hand-shake was painful. I could tell that even the tall and ever ebullient Nat was impressed as he blurted out 'we're both steam-ship men,' adding, 'from the Blue Funnel Line,' as if to compensate for our obvious short-comings.

'First-rate company,' Tomkins said. 'Nothing to be ashamed of. I gather we'll be handling a barque. You'll soon get the hang of it.'

I was less sure of this but further conversation was terminated by the lovely Doris who arrived to summon us to the presence. We travelled up in the lift to your father's office where, once again, he and Hanslip were waiting for us. Three chairs were arranged in a half-circle before your dad's desk and he wasted no time in briefing us.

'Well gentlemen,' he began, 'congratulations on your appointments. I won't expatiate on your individual virtues, but Commander Hanslip and I have our reasons for selecting you. The Commander will fill you in later this morning on the detail, but I'll brief you now' I remember he looked at his watch and I thought: 'this chap's got a newspaper to get out…'

Anyway, he explained what all this was about in fairly flattering terms regarding our success in being appointed to a vessel that he had especially bought for a voyage to the Arctic. 'You'll all have heard about the Andrée expedition,' he began and I have to confess I had no idea what he was talking about. 'And you'll know it disappeared somewhere north of Spitsbergen sometime in 1897. Its mysterious disappearance caused a lot of heart-ache in Sweden, somewhat akin to the loss of Scot and his companions in Antarctica did here in 1912.

'About three months ago,' he went on to say, 'I was approached by Madame Blavatskoya, the well-known White Russian medium whose remarkable talents have allowed many of us to communicate with those lost on the Somme and elsewhere. She told me she knew of the location of Salomon Andrée and his fellows; that it would be an act of great human compassion to recover the bodies and ease the national ignorance of the Swedes, and that such an act would redound to the credit of Great Britain. Being a newspaperman,' he added with a smile that I suppose was intended to find an understanding in our comprehension, 'only added to my desire to do it and to make a scoop.

'To this end I arranged for Commander Hanslip here to purchase a suitable vessel and have it dry-docked and fully refitted to his own specification. Some advice on the matter was forthcoming from my good friend Richard Holt,' here he looked at Nat and me, 'and as a result the ship now lies in the Surrey Commercial Dock and I am relying upon you gentlemen to get her up into the Arctic Ocean by the time the ice thaws and you can reach the location revealed to me by Madam Blavatskoya. As you will understand, this information is, at the present moment, under embargo, and I want it to be clearly understood that you are working for me personally and that you owe me a certain loyalty not to disclose any of this to anyone, not even your nearest and dearest. To this end I have avoided drawing attention to the vessel which is not, alas, renamed 'Courier,' as I should have liked, but retains her old name: *Alert*. However, once you are on your way, *The Courier* will bear a notice of your departure and I shall manage the flow of news personally to create the desired effect. To get the copy back here I have a man from the Marconi Company joining and one of my staff reporters and a photographer will also be joining you, so a couple of stops will furnish me with some photographs to whet the public's appetite.

'Owing to the necessity of preparing the vessel properly you three have to know all this before-hand, but no-one outside this room has any idea what we are about. As far as the dock-yard company were concerned the vessel is a scientific expedition going to examine certain magnetic anomalies in the waters of the Davis Strait. I have, however, asked the President and Council of the Royal Geographical and the Royal Zoological Societies if they would like to send anyone north this summer with a view to carrying out general observations and they suggested observations of the Northern Right Whale among other low-key matters which would provide experience for a party of three scientists who will, I am given to understand, be drawn from one or other or our universities.

'As far as all other plans are concerned, Commander Hanslip has the matter in hand and you will take all directions from him as he will be in full charge of the expedition. Any questions may be directed to him shortly. All I now require from you,' and here your father picked up a typed document from his desk, pressed the intercom buzzer to bring the lovely Doris into his office, and concluded, 'is your signatures as to the confidentiality of your service.'

Without any further debate we all obediently rose, scanned the brief document the wording of which swore us to secrecy, signed our names and stood and watched as Doris witnessed them all. I noticed that she gave Nat more than one glance and guessed that he had made a mental note of her address. It turned out that I was not wrong!

Then Hanslip had us all file out and reassemble in some sort of a broom-cupboard-cum-store-room where he gave us each a brown envelope.

'I want you, Tomkins, on board as soon as possible.'

'Aye, aye,' replied Tomkins taking one end of the envelope,

the traditional 'sir' conspicuous by its absence.

'Aye, aye, *sir*,' responded Hanslip, still retaining his grip on the other end. 'We may as well start as we intend to go on,' he added, perhaps catching something in Alan Tomkins's eye.

'Yes indeed, we may, in which case I am *Mister* Tomkins.' For a moment the two men stood in a rather ridiculous tableau, both glaring at one another, a thin brown envelope between them. They were both of a similar height, both ruddy in complexion and I felt an almost prescient sensation that I was witnessing the beginnings of a long-running tussle as to primacy – but perhaps that too I have added in the years that have passed since that afternoon. One never quite knows where memory is concerned.

Eventually Hanslip grinned, with patent insincerity I think I can say with a certain amount of conviction, and let go of his end of the envelope. 'Of course, *Mr* Tomkins.' He turned to me and Nat. '*Mr* Adams and *Mr* Gardner, your special orders. If you two could be aboard by the end of the week your accommodation should be ready by then.

And that is how the three of us found ourselves shipmates aboard your Daddy's yacht.

*

It's getting late, d'you want me to go on? All right.

*

When I got aboard that Thursday evening, picking my way over the greased steel wire ropes and the general muck that accumulates on the deck of a vessel newly out of dry-dock, the first figure to greet me was the ship-keeper. He reminded me of the narrator so frequently employed in the short stories of W.W. Jacobs, though he was less obliging and to my question as to where Mr Tomkins might be found he merely jerked his thumb over his shoulder and left me to find my own way down into what turned out to be a surprisingly cosy, mahogany-panelled saloon that I knew instinctively Hanslip would soon be calling 'the ward-room'. Tomkins was not there but he had heard me and hailed me from his cabin, one of several that opened off the saloon and was separated by a sliding door.

'Come in.' He gestured for me to sit on the bunk, indicated half a dozen bottles of India Pale Ale, a bottle-opener and excused himself for a few minutes. I opened a bottle and drank out of it while he finished some paper-work, a fact he indicated by blowing out his cheeks, turning to me with a smile and reaching for a bottle of IPA.

'Well, here we are,' he said pleasantly, raising his bottle to chink mine. He sat in his collar-less shirt sleeves, his blue serge trousers held up by both belt and braces – a sailing-ship man to his finger-tips. 'So, on the basis that we may as well start as we mean to go on,' he announced in a tone of mock gravity, 'what are we to call ourselves, Mr Adams?'

'I'm happy to call you whatever you wish: "sir," "chief," "Mr Tomkins"…' I ran out of options.

'How about Alan?'

I think I grinned. 'I'm Ned, short for Edward, but please not Ted. I'm pretty sure Nat Gardner will fall in line.'

'He'll have to,' Tomkins said. 'Ned and Nat. The crew'll have some fun with that. Better use rank in front of them. Chief, Second and Third…' He paused for a moment, then ran on, 'I expect our esteemed leader will cling to his naval rank. I noticed we are all engaged as "officers" rather than "mates," though both he and the rest of us will have to sign the Articles as master and mates.'

'He's a reservist, I presume,' I said. 'My instructions said that uniform would be worn once we left British waters.'

'Yes. I take it you have one. I've had to pay Silver's a visit though, to be fair, the charge will be reimbursed. It's all part of the mystery, but once we appear off the Norwegian coast and the news is out, we have to make a good showing. His Nibs has obviously given all this a good deal of thought.'

'Or Commander Hanslip has insisted,' I added.

Alan Tomkins laughed. 'Yeah. I had the unhappy experience of working with his type during the Great War. I hope we can cure him of the worst excesses they seem to indulge in and rub along together.'

'I hope so too.'

'Seen anything of Nat?' Tomkins asked, giving the shortened form of Gardner's name a certain flourish to match the larger-than-life chap to whom it applied.

'No, sorry.'

'Oh well. He's got until tomorrow, but we need him here soon, there's a good deal to be done and he needs to sign the Articles by then. The crew sign-on on Monday morning and if all goes well we'll be off by this time next weekend. Have you signed-on?' I shook my head. 'Dock Street tomorrow morning then. Hanslip's opened them, you can pop in at nine and then get back here for morning smoke-o. I want those topgallant yards sent up tomorrow. A good introduction to sail, or a re-run of school-days. She only carries a thimble-full of steam coal…'

'What about engineers?'

'Monday. I've poached some from my last ship which was not a sailing ship but was sold to the Belgians under our feet. Good men going to waste.'

'You were master?'

'Perceptive of you. Yes indeed I was; Master under God, Mr Adams, until He deserted me…' he paused for a moment, looking round his hutch of a cabin. 'Still, this is a bit out of the ordinary, though I have no faith in this Blavatskoya nonsense.' I forbore correcting him. 'Anyway,' he went on, 'there's an interesting folio of charts on the bridge. That's your domain, so perhaps you can tell me where we are off to just by guessing.

According to the rather spare information in my secret orders, the old bat Blavatskoya said something about a white island. I thought that rather rich since most islands in the Arctic, and there seem to be rather a lot of them, will be white. Any ideas?'

'No, none whatsoever. As I had a day to kick my heels I did think of making enquiries at the RGS…'

'RGS?'

'Royal Geographical Society…'

'Ah yes, of course, stupid of me.'

'But then I thought I might give the game away and that all would be revealed in time…'

Our chat was interrupted by a clatter on the companionway and a booming 'Anyone at home?' Two minutes later Nat Gardner had joined me on the chief officer's bunk with one of Tomkins's bottles in his over-large fist. I seem to recollect another half an hour's fairly aimless chat at the end of which Tomkins announced that since we now owed him a drink we should all go ashore to the nearest pub and find something to eat. During a pretty indigestible meat pie, peas and mashed potatoes, Tomkins told us that he wanted us both to take advantage of the ship being dead over the weekend and get to know her, particularly her rigging. 'I'll walk you round and you can watch the t'gallants going aloft. If you've got any balls you can go up yourselves and check the riggers seize all the shackles pins and secure the foot-ropes and Flemish horses. Between you you'd better check the seizings on the shroud battens too,' he went on. I recalled the solid wooden battens that crossed the vessel's shrouds in place of ratlines, making going aloft much easier, even if it did increase windage and looked clumsy. I found myself thankful for that. He finished off with something to the effect that he'd like to get the ship in good order before the Old Man arrived, adding that that wouldn't be 'until he's got running hot water and a hot and running steward.'

After a bare breakfast of coffee and toast, the following morning found Gardner and I on deck in a fresh breeze under a grey sky. 'This ain't no Indian Ocean,' Nat said out of the corner of his mouth as we watched the riggers prepare the fore-topgallant yard for running aloft. It was a long wooden spar, spruce, I supposed, lighter by far than the lower yards, which were of steel, but it was secured to the upmost section of the foremast by its parrel by lunch time, along with most of its gear – braces, lifts and so forth - and was followed in the afternoon by the main topgallant. Back in the pub that evening Tomkins declared himself satisfied with the day's work and asked us a few rudimentary questions about the running gear, to see to what degree we had profited from our labours. Thanks not merely due to the day's travail but also to my *Conway* training, I proved up to this catechism. Gardner, who had attended the *Worcester*, our rival training ship on the Thames, also passed this *viva voce* examination with ease. I wondered vaguely if my father could have understood the complexities of the rigging of a sailing ship, but soon forgot him when Nat announced that he was going 'up west' the following evening.

'You have a floosie in tow, or shall you be trawling?'

'Ha, ha,' grinned Nat, tapping the side of his nose with his index-finger.

'I'm not joking, Mr Gardner,' Tomkins said, suddenly serious and pulling a pipe from his pocket. 'As far as I know there's no doctor on this voyage and if you cop a dose of something unpleasant, you'll have to submit to my ministrations.'

'I intend taking the charming Doris for a turn around the floor at the Café Royal.'

I laughed and Tomkins stopped tamping the tobacco in his pipe-bowl. 'Who?'

'His Lordship's private secretary,' I said, half enviously, half admiringly. 'I noticed her giving you the glad-eye.'

'Stone the crows,' said Tomkins before resuming the interminable fiddling that pipe-smokers find so absorbing.

'Still,' I said, probably with some residual half-thought about my own father, 'given he's providing everything else on this expedition, I'm surprised Southmoore's not giving us a doctor. Wasn't there some talk about bringing bodies back?'

'Good Lord, yes. I had clean forgotten about that,' admitted Tomkins, excusing himself by adding, 'had my eye on too many other concerns getting the ship ready.'

'I hope he doesn't expect us to…'

'There'll be someone to attend to that,' said Nat confidently.

'How d'you know,' we began before both of us knew the answer. 'You've already wined and dined the lovely Doris who has revealed all,' I guessed.

Nat grinned. 'Well, I know a good deal more than you chaps about the Andrée expedition. Apparently after this weird White Russian contacted her boss she had to prepare a note about it all. She knows pretty much everything about our mission, it seems, though I was sworn to secrecy over my entrée,' he grinned again.

'Well, who is this Andrée fellow? I was under the impression that this was a Swedish matter, though Andrée sounds distinctly French. His Lordship mentioned Sweden, didn't he?' asked Tomkins.

'Yes, but he mentioned Andrée too,' I said. We both looked expectantly at Nat.

'He was a Swede and in 1897, with backing from Alfred Nobel, he undertook to fly over the North Pole in a balloon with two others. They left from Spitsbergen and simply disappeared. After they had vanished all sorts of stories circulated. It was their second attempt, they were ill-prepared – Doris mentioned they took evening dress and champagne, intending to land near the Pole and drink the health of the King of Sweden/Norway as it was then. Several search expeditions were launched, apparently, in Greenland, Siberia and around Spitsbergen, but nothing was found. Then this barmy Russian woman…'

'His Lordship doesn't think Madame Blavatskoya is barmy,' I interjected mischievously. In fact I entirely agreed with Nat, but felt we should try and take the matter seriously.

'Is that it?' Tomkins asked. 'That's your excuse for joining the ship late?'

'I wasn't late,' responded a suddenly deflated Nat.

'You were later than Ned here.'

'Well, if I hadn't been late you wouldn't have a clue what we were about to embark upon.'

'I am about to embark upon six or more months of fully paid employment,' Tomkins said, extinguishing the umpteenth match and dropping it into the ash-tray. 'Ours not to reason why…'

I remember the weekend that followed as one of those odd periods that will be familiar to all ships' officers. The vessel was dead with all but the three of us on board, plus the old ship-keeper who kept his own counsel and emerged like a badger after sunset, and any casual labour we employed, such as the riggers and the last of the dry-dock labourers who made a vain attempt to finish the paint and varnish work and clear our decks in decidedly inclement weather. At the end of the working day these men knocked-off, of course, and the *Alert* fell silent and the cold seeped back into her as night fell. Our food was inadequate and our evening meals in that pub, the name of which I have forgotten, were monotonous and dreadful. I could have gone home, but that did not seem fair on Alan Tomkins, so we left Nat to make an attempt on the virtue of Doris and got down to the serious business of preparation. In that sense the weekend was a little oasis of contentment. Despite the cold, the lack of food or crew, there were tasks to undertake and we undertook them, working through a list Tomkins drew up and many tasks of which were entirely practical. I found I got on with Alan Tomkins. He might have been a difficult man to deal with since he had so recently been in command of his own ship, but he seemed to bear the world no ill-will and simply got on with what required his attention: the complete professional.

With all the yards crossed I made a point of ascending both the fore and main masts and working my way out to each yard-arm so that I could identify all the ropes, lines and chains that made up the lifts, braces, sheets, tacks and so on. In truth the little barque was not over complex, for her two forward masts only carried courses, upper and lower topsails and a single topgallant, while her mizen carried a gaff headed spanker with a triangular topsail that ran vertically up the mizen topmast on a jackstay. It was pretty clear she would be no flyer under sail, though she had a pretty clipper-bow and a gilded fiddle-head. Her bow-sprit and jib-boom carried three sails, a foretopmast stay-sail and an inner and an outer jib, and she set a couple of staysails between the masts.

Down on deck I tried to cram into my head the location of the belaying pins to which each one led, so that I might find them at sea, in the dark. The rigging itself had a logic, the layout of the belaying pins, though standard to British merchant sailing vessels, took some mastering. Alan Tomkins assured me that others would usually be around to attend to the detail, but I was driven by the desire not to be outdone. Somehow that quizzing by Hanslip over my lack of square-rig experience during the process of my interview had exposed an ignorance I was oddly ashamed of. Anyway, by the time our odd little idyll came to an end on Monday morning, and new faces began to appear with remarkable speed, I was reasonably competent *and* confident.

I had signed-on in Dock Street as Tomkins had bid me on the Friday. There were two oddities with which I was not familiar about this; the first was that I discovered that I was signing-on a vessel registered as a yacht – perfectly understandable under the circumstances and not, in itself, of any note. Your father was a member of several prestigious yacht clubs but was unable to fly fancy ensigns without drawing attention to the vessel, so we sailed under some club of which Hanslip was a member, eschewed any burgee and would wear the common-or-garden red duster of a merchantman. The second odd thing was that in signing-on that Friday, the first time I encountered the remainder of the crew was as they came aboard in dribs and drabs the following Monday afternoon, most of the firemen and seamen the worse for wear. Nothing new in that, of course, though, ironically it marked us more a merchantman than a yacht! As for Hanslip, our Old Man, he arrived in a car around eleven and immediately announced an officer's conference in the saloon at noon. It was, he added, the time that a proper ship's routine would start, the ensign would be hoisted, officers would commence deck-watches and – his words, not mine – 'the routines and discipline of a well-run vessel would prevail'.

As far as the crew was concerned no such thing was likely to occur much before we got to sea, but the officers, engineers, the Marconi man, the scientists – who all looked like undergraduates – and a rather elderly gent who turned out to be a doctor, all obeyed. Your father must have had a late change of heart, or perhaps your dad was moved to an act of charity as our quack seemed to have enjoyed better days and bore no resemblance to my father. Southmoore's staff reporter and photographer were not expected until the afternoon we were due to sail on the high-water and were, in fact, late. We had actually left the berth and an instruction that they were to join us at Blyth, our last coaling port, but they made-it in a taxi while we were going through the lock and so joined by a 'pier-head jump,' which seemed to amuse them if it infuriated Hubert

Henry Hanslip.

Anyway, I have run ahead of my narrative. H.H.H, had us all – the officers, that is - assembled in the saloon that Monday forenoon and welcomed us all, even though all of us had joined the vessel before him. He pointed out that we were bound upon a scientific expedition and hoped to return by the autumn. In the unlikely event of being trapped in the ice and forced to winter in high latitudes, we would receive a lump sum above our pay in compensation. No mention was made of the recovery of bodies, of Madame Blavatskoya, or Mr Andrée, and it was clear that only the three of us, plus Hanslip, had any inkling of the truth behind Lord Southmoore's project, though it turned out later that the old quack did. Indeed, it was quickly apparent that, until the journalist and the photographer jumped aboard, no-one beyond this privileged quintet knew of the connection with *The Courier*, though our actual departure was photographed by an unobtrusive young man with a large plate camera who had been given permission to come on board and take some evocative shots of our rig and the curious collection of individuals accumulating on board. Someone said he worked for the *Woolwich Gazette*, or the *Tilbury Times*; others that he was a ship-lover curious about our not so lofty spars – an increasing rarity on the Thames. Anyway, as cover it worked well. Southmoore got some good shots of the ship preparing for her voyage. Expedition vessels like ours were few and far between after the Great War and we carried about us a little of the glamour of Scott, Shackleton and Worsley, who had himself made such a voyage the year before.

Anyway, the crew spent the next couple of days washing down paintwork and sending the sails up. We didn't get the filth off the deck until we got into the river, but it was now and in the next few days that the companions with whom we would share our lives for the next few months made their appearance. I can now only properly recall those who became significant in what followed. Among the assembly of officers in the saloon, besides Hanslip and we three mates, Dr Crichton proved to be a dry old stick in every sense of the word and our chief engineer, Owen Jones, a Welshman of memorable rotundity and an equable temperament such that I have never come across in any man, before or since. He simply loved life, even the sea-life, which he regarded with what in any other man would be a suspect geniality and seemed incapable of being defeated by life's trials. He had been recruited by Alan Tomkins when Hanslip asked Tomkins if he knew of a decent and reliable chief engineer and they were old ship-mates. Jones's assistant, the second engineer, was a diminutive Geordie named Rayne who, one felt, might collapse at any moment, such was the fragility of his physical appearance; in fact he proved incredibly tough, utterly suited to life in the ferocious heats of a boiler-room, though the Arctic cold would test him. Others I can introduce as they appear in the narrative, their characters had less to do with the outcome of our voyage, though the Bosun, a Cockney seaman whose name escapes me, was a tower of strength and soon after our departure licked his deck-hands into a half-decent ship's company. There were a dozen of them altogether, a very generous complement for a small auxiliary barque like ours, varying from several able-seamen, all of whom had served in sail, down to one deck-boy, James Dell, fresh out of a school in Poplar. Since we would not spend all our time under steam, the engine room boasted just three greasers, the boiler-room three firemen and a trimmer. The deckhands had signed an agreement to assist 'with the machinery if and when required.' Apart from the Bosun, we also carried a carpenter, a tall North Chinese named Mr Wang who spoke excellent English and lived in Limehouse.

Our wants were attended to by a steward, a cook and a boy,

Hanslip himself attending to the vessel's victualing stores for reasons of petty aggrandisement. I got the impression his relationship with the steward was one of long-standing.

As for Hanslip, he was full of himself. He handed out specially made cap-badges to we three mates. They bore *The Courier*'s winged Hermes in gold wire in a similarly wrought wreath of laurel surmounted by the naval crown and must have cost a bob-or-two but I suspected they were as far as he could go in setting the sort of tone he envisaged, having been denied a blue ensign or a club burgee in the interests of secrecy. After a rather boring pep-talk of the kind I had heard aboard the *Conway*, he dismissed the meeting with the caveat: 'deck officers stand fast,' which was a bit over-the-top since we were seated but with the saloon cleared and the hovering steward kicked out of the adjacent pantry and all doors secured, he addressed Alan Tomkins, Nat Gardner and myself.

'Still can't tell you much,' he confided, 'but it's no secret to you gentlemen that we're bound north towards Spitsbergen. The vessel's cleared outwards for Blyth and Norwegian ports, chiefly Bergen and perhaps Tromso and/or the Lofotens, anyway we'll see. Much will depend upon the weather and our coal situation.

'Now, I know you chaps have had no experience in polar seas, but I was in North Russia after the war with the naval forces supporting the Allied Intervention in nineteen and twenty, so if any of you are entertaining any anxieties on that score I can put them to rest.' I remember him looking at each of the three of us as if expecting some murmur of appreciation, but he was out of luck. As if disappointed and seeking some sort of reaction, he went on, patting the saloon table, 'the ship's sound, heavily constructed as a sealer, ice strengthened forrard as you will have noted. As to her running, well, I want a smart ship; smart ships are happy ships…' at this point I could almost hear Nat Gardner laughing, even quoting the dictum alongside our oh-so-serious commander, the words being a well-remembered chant with which the authorities running training ships like the *Worcester* and *Conway* justified the petty rules, the oppressive discipline, the dreadful food and the vicious corporal punishment meted out to over exuberant youth.

Anyway, it was all over at last and Hanslip rose and picked up his cap with its oak-leaf embossed peak, ostentatiously laid on the table before him as he had sat down and bearing the then unfamiliar new cap-badge.

'You two,' he said, pointing at Nat and me, 'can come aft while we raise the ensign.' I supposed he referred to our being familiar with the drill of saluting from our training-ship days, something he assumed Alan Tomkins knew nothing about. I caught the mate's wry smile at being relieved of this small ceremony, but I knew better than Hanslip.

Apart from the stupid drama of the pier-head jump of the journalist, Geoffrey Hardacre, and the photographer, John Sykes, our departure was unremarkable. Our Trinity House Pilot saw us down-stream, disembarking off the Sunk lightvessel off Harwich about two o'clock in the afternoon. He gave us the customary wave from the pilot-cutter's little motor-boat as he departed and called up to me – I was leaning over the rail to see him off – that we looked like 'a bloody jumble-sale.'

As soon as we had lifted the pilot-ladder Commander Hanslip handed the ship over to me as it was my watch, the twelve-to-four. After a blustery week we found ourselves in a North Sea bereft of a breath of wind, so we proceeded north under power. Once clear of the Shipway which led us out of the sand-banks which make the navigation of the outer estuary of the Thames such a nightmare, we settled down and I had a couple of hours to take stock, pacing up and down the tiny wheelhouse with just an able seaman on the wheel for company.

Steam-ships are quiet and with no wind, the only noise was the swish of our forward progress and the creak of a gear aloft as the little *Alert* rolled very gently in a low swell. It is a curious fact that seafarers never know what their ship looks like at sea and it was only much later, when I saw some photos taken by *The Courier*'s discreet photographer that I had any inkling of precisely to what our pilot had referred.

I have already described our rig, that of a three-masted barque, very economical on man-power, but it was our decks that looked most like a jumble-sale. It was quite clear that Old Southmoore – sorry, your father – had given H.H.H. an open cheque-book when he was drawing up the specification for conversion, for no expense had been spared to turn this elderly wooden sealer – she'd been built in 1891 in Dundee – into a half-decent expedition-ship. Even the pokey glory-hole of a fo'c's'le for the deck crew under the small well-deck forward had been extended and ran aft on either side of the hatch. This was trunked down to a capacious hold, a gloomy cavern that stretched aft under the small raised centre-castle which incorporated all the officers' and specialists' cabins, the galley, a small workshop for the carpenter and the wireless shack, the proud domain of the Marconi man from Chelmsford. Apart from general stores, lockers and, at the bottom, fresh-water in galvanised steel tanks, the hold had a 'tween-deck-cum-sail locker. The hold-spaces were serviced by a swinging derrick which had its heel goose-necked to the foremast but required the standing rigging on the side you wished to use to be slackened off, which was a pain in the backside. On top of the hatch we carried a small pram-dinghy and abaft the wheel-house and flying bridge, which was actually not very high, there nestled a pair of lifeboats, bloody difficult to swing out on their radial davits owing to the running rigging belayed along the ship's rail. However, we had plenty of alternatives. On top of the galley and wireless-shack we carried a dory and a smart little clinker sailing dinghy, and on skids over the after well-deck a pair of large boats, a pulling-cutter and a motor launch. As if that was not enough another dory was slung on its side and lashed in the mizen chains to port and to starboard, similarly secured, was a smaller pulling-gig.

The boiler and engine rooms together with the coal bunkers occupied almost the entire after third of the ship, all except for some confined spaces under the counter which provided extra storage space and access to the well into which the banjo frame lifted the screw. This was an ingenious device which allowed us to uncouple the propeller-shaft and draw it up into the hull, useful if making a long passage under sail (it reduced drag), or to avoid damage if caught in ice.

I'm sorry, I'm rambling, but the truth was, that as I stood there that afternoon running up towards the Aldeburgh Napes, I found I had grown rather fond of the quirky little vessel and I distinctly recall this somewhat cosy sensation – a jolly good one for any seaman off on such an unorthodox trip as we were then embarking – with a second and sudden damper, a feeling that all was not quite right. Quite unbidden the expression 'ship of fools' floated into my mind.

At first I tried to dismiss it as a silly anxiety. Alan Tomkins was right; we had work, a contract for six months and a bonus if things went wrong and we got delayed in the ice. I think it was that cautionary clause that triggered by misgivings but it occurred to me that, despite appearances and a certain sense of bravado, none of us were Scotts, let alone Shackletons or Worsleys. Commander Hanslip's assertions about having been in Russian waters during the Allied Intervention in the civil war that followed the Revolution of October nineteen seventeen was actually a very slender claim to Arctic experience. As far as I knew the British naval presence was only through the summer months and actually had only a small amount of contact with ice. He would actually have been more reassuring had he claimed having been in the Baltic trade where ice navigation was common and I was certain sure that several of the weather-beaten old devils who had occupied that waiting-room at *The Courier*'s head office were of that ilk. Which, of course, led me to the presumption that Hanslip had selected his three executive officers on the grounds that they knew less than he did, though having chosen Nat and myself purely on such reasoning, he clearly needed Tomkins for his experience in sail. That boded ill, as had that little spat in the broom-cupboard. Such things as how we addressed each other may seem silly, but they established a certain standard, a regime, if you like, to which we ought all to have signed-up as much as we signed-on the official Articles of Agreement prescribed by His Majesty's Board of Trade.

It turned out that I had got it spot-on and it was not long before the first sign of trouble emerged.

I think we had better leave it there for tonight.

THE SECOND EVENING - THE SHIP OF FOOLS

As far as we three mates were aware we were bound for Spitsbergen by way of Blyth, Bergen and possibly Tromso or the Lofoten Islands. Hanslip had indicated, with a certain smug importance that our 'secret orders' – by which we all assumed Madame Blavatskoya's divinations would be revealed to us - would be opened once we departed from Blyth. So-far-so-good. Unfortunately the first spat on board was predictably between Hanslip and Tomkins. I didn't witness it, but Nat did because he had just relieved Alan at eight o'clock the following morning. Before he went down for his breakfast after keeping the four-to-eight, Tomkins was writing up the fair-copy log-book from the slate that we kept in the chart-room when our gallant commander stormed onto the bridge.

During my middle watch – midnight to four in the morning - a gentle breeze had sprung up from the sou'west and by half past five it had filled-in. As soon as the off-watch hands were called for wash-down routine, the first proper scrub our decks received, Alan sent them aloft to cast off the gaskets and twenty minutes later, with the engine still sending us along at six or seven knots, he had got our passage speed up to ten or eleven by setting the fore and main courses, all four topsails and both t'gallants. It was this act of seamanlike initiative that Hanslip fulminated against.

According to Nat the conversation went something like this:

'What the hell d'you think you're doing Three-Oh,' Three-Oh being Hanslip's informal mode of addressing the Third Officer (I was Two-Oh and Tomkins was, of course, Number One). Nat looked perplexed.

'You've set sail!' Hanslip expostulated, but before Nat could explain, Tomkins came out of the chart-room.

'I set sail, sir, at 06.00 this morning…'

'Without my orders!'

Well, there was nothing in the night orders that said I couldn't or shouldn't set sail, Commander Hanslip, a fair wind had come up and…'

'You do nothing on this ship without my orders!' Hanslip raged, almost beside himself. 'Just because you've commanded a merchantman yourself doesn't mean you can assume responsibilities that are properly mine,' he roared.

Alan Tomkins flushed deeply and responded. 'I didn't think the matter warranted your being told, sir…'

'You bloody well tell me…' but he got no further as Tomkins persisted with his own line of argument.

'And I'd be obliged, Commander Hanslip, if you find my conduct displeases you, you berated me in private. I have a strong prejudice against being addressed in such a manner that reflects my personal circumstances in front of junior officers and…' - here apparently Tomkins jerked his head towards the wheel-house where one of the able-seamen was at the wheel and vastly enjoying the contre-temps, the relating of which in the fo'c'sle later he was already rehearsing, I imagine - 'and members of the crew. It is extremely bad for discipline.'

Nat said this last was uttered with such an air of authority mixed with a tone of utter contempt, that it stopped Hanslip in his tracks.

Taking advantage of the hiatus, Tomkins added. 'I'm going below for my breakfast. If you wish to speak to me on the subject I shall be in my cabin in about half an hour. In the mean time I am sure Mr Gardner here will pass word to shorten down. Good morning.'

And Nat, unfazed by this public disagreement, coolly enquired if he should take sail off the barque.

'It was only a force four,' he told me when I relieved him at noon, 'and right on our port quarter, but the silly bugger had to save his face. Looking round the horizon he said: "It'll freshen further within the hour, Mister, we've a new crew, get the t'gallants off her pronto". And now look,' Nat had gestured at the grey sea through which the *Alert* scended with an easy motion, 'three hours later and what? A four still? Certainly nothing to get excited about.'

I learned later that day from Owen Jones that there had been a little sequel in the saloon where Hanslip, having stood on the bridge while Nat ordered the t'gallants clewed up in their gear and a couple of men sent up both masts to secure them, eventually arrived in what he indeed called the wardroom for his own breakfast. Tomkins and Jones had just finished theirs and were laughing companionably together and Hanslip assumed that the former had been telling the latter about the incident.

Hanslip affected not to notice, ordered his breakfast and ate it in silence. When the two others rose to leave – they were the last officers to break their fasts that morning both just having come off watch – he told Tomkins he would see him in his, Hanslip's, cabin in twenty minutes. Precisely what happened next I can only surmise from a few remarks Tomkins let slip later and it all sounded rather childish. Apparently Hanslip declared that there was only room for one captain and Tomkins agreed and said there was nothing in the night orders that precluded the use of his own initiative in making sail, that the coal bunkers were finite in their capacity and the wind, when fair, was not to be sneezed at. Hanslip, still fighting to save face, snapped that Tomkins shouldn't try and be smart, at which point Tomkins shrugged his shoulders and made to leave the cabin. Hanslip let him go but called after him that he should mind his manners to his superior officer.

Tomkins told me about this on the first morning after we had left Blyth, when he was relieving me at O-four hundred, having scrutinised Hanslip's night orders.

'I think that we're going to have trouble with the Old Man, Ned my lad,' he said quietly. 'Either that. Or I am going to have to quit; I thought about it while we were in Blyth but…' he shrugged, 'it's a job and with mouths to feed I need the money.'

This was the first allusion Alan had made to having dependants. I didn't press him at the time, but I gathered he had an ailing mother and a sister who took care of her. Both relied upon Alan as bread-winner.

*

I don't remember much about our short stay in Blyth, though two things stuck out. The first was that two hands got drunk and Nat was sent to bail them out. Nothing unusual about that but it upset Hanslip who seemed to have lost some of his glossy polish. Certainly the ship did, as she was covered in a fine layer of black coal-dust. With full bunkers, we even had bags of the stuff stowed on the after deck and shoved a few tons down the hold forward by way of a reserve.

The other thing was the discretion shown by *The Courier*'s staff reporter, or 'Special Correspondent,' Geoffrey Hardacre, and his side-kick, the photographer, John Sykes. When a news-hound from the local rag came sniffing round the gangway, Hardacre chased him away, fobbing him off with some cock-and-bull nonsense that we were going north to prospect for lead and other minerals on Jan Mayen Island. Old Southmoore certainly had secured a pair of loyal adherents in his own private team, but after Alan Tomkins's comments that first morning and the odd meeting Hanslip called in the saloon as soon as we had cleared the land after leaving Blyth, I began to wonder how he had settled on Hanslip.

I had mentioned our brief exchange to Gardner when he relieved me that midnight, just to put him on the *qui vive* really, relative to Hanslip. I was more disturbed than I can say about what Tomkins had told me because I thought him, Tomkins that is, a very decent, steady chap who had taken demotion from Master down to Chief Mate in his stride. It was common enough in those very tough days, but it took character to wear it lightly, especially when goaded over it and Hanslip seemed to have provoked him, though I only have his version of what went on. Anyway, I had taken an instant liking to Alan, largely due to that short weekend we had worked together in the Surrey Commercial Dock and it didn't take me long to realise that he, like Nat Gardner, was a man of parts. Like a number of merchant marine officers, both were well-read, Alan exceptionally so, as the collection of books on his small cabin book-shelf attested, literary works sitting alongside the standard reference books any master-mariner would take with him to sea.

If we did 'have trouble with the Old Man,' I did not want Alan chucking his hand in, though he would have to do it before we left the Norwegian coast. Such an eventuality would make my life and Nat's well-nigh intolerable, and concede some sort of a victory to Hanslip. From what little I had seen of our gallant Commander I did not relish the prospect of that. Anyway, it seemed sensible just to pass on Alan's warning to Nat, if only to present a united front if it ever came to push of pike, so to speak, but Nat came up with an analysis of his own which was uncomfortably close to mine.

'This is all a bit of rum do, isn't it?' he remarked. 'I mean Hanslip is odd enough and frankly I don't think that service as a reserve officer in the Allied Intervention qualifies one for Arctic work, though it might just about provide a few insights. And we three mates, not one of us knows diddly-squat about ice navigation. I applied for the job out of a sense of adventure; this sort of thing won't come along very often nowadays, but I expected to be shipping out with grizzled old Dundee men who'd served their time in whalers or sealers from the east coast of Scotland. There were at least three of them in that waiting room in Fleet Street…'

'Were there?' I interjected, surprised at the depth of Nat's insight.

He nodded. 'Yes. I got talking to one of them while you were having your interview; you went in first, if you recall. Anyway, at the very least I thought we would ship an ice-pilot but…' he shrugged, 'nothing of the sort. Instead we get a quasi-naval product of the Great War who clearly chose thee and me on the grounds that we were from the *Conway* and the *Worcester* and, given what you say, I reckon old Southmoore insisted on Mr Tomkins as Chief Officer so that his ship was in a safe pair of hands.'

I hadn't thought of that; Gardner was shrewd for his years and I looked at him sharply. 'You think that?' I asked. 'Then why choose Hanslip as Commander in the first place?'

'Well, either Hanslip has some claim on his Lordship or Southmoore wanted a front man. Hanslip's naval rank adds a touch of distinction, and he's got some sort of decoration, that ribbon he wears, I don't know what it is, but from the point of view of publicity my guess is he's the gilt on the ginger-bread-work. Don't forget Southmoore's a news-paper baron on a mission, not a stingy ship-owner. I don't know what his outlay is in mounting this expedition as a consequence of some bloody séance in Hampstead or Highgate, but it must be considerable…'

'I've heard one hundred thousand mentioned…'

Nat whistled through his teeth. 'Christ on a bike! Well, he won't understand the dynamics that pertain on board and my guess is that he's tied the Old Man up with so many instructions that Hanslip doesn't quite know which way to jump.'

'Well, if you're right this voyage is likely to be a farce or a disaster and frankly I'd rather it was a farce.'

'We'll find out tomorrow morning,' Nat responded, 'or at least you and everyone else will, I shall be on watch, but I gather there's a three-line whip out for the officers, engineers and super-numeraries to assemble in the saloon – er, wardroom – at 10.30 hours.'

'You'd better turn in,' I said.

'You've seen the Old Man's night orders,' Nat said, straightening up from where he had been leaning companionably on the rail and slapped the teak barrier that ran round the bridge, a dark, circumscribing line against white paintwork.

'Yup,' I responded, having read and signed the Order Book before seeking Nat out on the bridge-wing. 'Call him if the wind changes in velocity or direction.'

'Well good-night,' he said and a moment later he had gone below, leaving me looking up at the night sky. The moon was up, a waxing crescent, and a dusting of cloud showed a steady sou'sou'westerly breeze. The engines were shut down and we were steering a course for Bergen under all plain sail. Beyond that, I, as navigator, knew only that we would then head 'towards' Spitsbergen; 'towards' in the old sailing-ship manner, meaning that was the intention but much lay in the lap of the gods. Quite how much we had yet to find out.

*

Half-past ten the following forenoon found Alan Tomkins and I, with the Chief and Second Engineers, Dr Crichton, Dave Manners, the Sparks from Marconi's, Geoffrey Hardacre and John Sykes, *The Courier*'s people and our three so called scientists, Bill Maddox, who was our meteorologist and oceanographer, Derek Cronshaw our geologist and Jim Doughty our naturalist. They were still an unknown quantity, rather like Ahab's whale-boat crew and thus far had kept themselves to themselves, largely due to feeling queasy, I think.

I was rubbing the sleep out of my eyes when I sat down at precisely 10.30, the five bells from the bridge ringing the half hour. Coffee was on the table and within seconds of my taking my place at the table between Alan Tomkins and Dr Crichton, Hanslip walked in with a chart rolled up under his arm. After some preliminary remarks about getting the ship properly cleaned-up after coaling, all of which were entirely unnecessary since Alan had seen to all that the previous day, he took a cigarette case from his pocket and, while we all waited in dutiful silence, he lit it.

'Now gentlemen,' he began, 'some of you know a little of our mission and while I am fully supportive of any programmes you wish to run,' here he looked pointedly at the three scientists, 'yours is not the primary function of this expedition.'

The three young men looked at each other with somewhat perplexed expressions as Hanslip moved on. 'Our main purpose is to locate the bodies and determine the fate of the Swedish *Ørnen* expedition, the so-called "flight of the eagle," which, led by Salomon August Andrée, left Danskøya, or Dane's Island, which lies here,' he unrolled the chart, spread it out and pointed to one of a cluster of islands that lay off the north-west corner of West Spitsbergen, 'on 11 July 1897. The *Ørnen* was a hydrogen-filled balloon and Andrée and his two companions were attempting to fly to the North Pole. After their departure, nothing was ever heard of them again.'

He paused as we digested this fact, or rather those to whom it was news digested it. I was eagerly awaiting the revelations of the famous Russian medium when Bill Maddox broke in with a question. 'But how the hell are we going to find this balloon and why, so long after the event…?'

'I'm coming to that, Mr Maddox…'

'*Doctor* Maddox, if it's all the same to you skipper…'

I sensed Alan Tomkins was enjoying the moment as Hanslip responded. 'I'm *Commander* Hanslip,' he said, hurrying on and stinging the young scientist as he did so. 'Now, as to the last part of your question, Maddox, Lord Southmoore considers it his duty to relieve the great anxiety and, it has to be said, curiosity that still clings to this tragedy in Sweden. There are those still alive who do not know what happened to their nearest and dearest and his Lordship conceives it an act of great national benevolence worthy of the greatest imperial maritime power the world has ever seen to clear up the mystery. As to where we shall be searching, well his Lordship has received certain intelligence the source of which remains a secret,' and here he unsubtly shot Alan and me a look which obviously abjured us to silence, 'that the three men died on an island somewhere to the east of the Svalbard Archipelago. The Norwegians, who administer the territory under a Treaty concluded under the auspices of the League of Nations in nineteen twenty or thereabouts, call it *Kvitøya*, or in English: White Island.'

'And there's only one?' ventured Maddox with the freedom of the academic in such stuffily pompous surroundings, though one might have expected him to know, given his position on our grand expedition. 'Strikes me there might be rather a lot of white islands up there,' he said, gesturing at the Admiralty chart of the Svalbard archipelago.

'There's only one that bears the name,' Hanslip said smoothly, drawing on his cigarette. 'Any questions?'

There was a babble of queries but I cannot recall what they were. Someone asked when we would be getting home, I seem to remember, I think it was the bird-watcher, Doughty, and someone else asked whether we were going to stop anywhere going north, to which Hanslip said yes, to take in victuals and land what he called 'despatches,' adding that 'there would be no shore-leave and if one word of this got out there would be consequences'. I wasn't taking much notice; I was more interest in skewing the chart from under Hanslip's nose so that I could have a look at the White Island.

That would be a good place to leave it for tonight, but I've a good deal of ground to cover so, if it's all right with you I'll press on with the trip from Bergen, northwards.

*

Alas, my memory isn't perfect and unfortunately I lost my private journal after my wife...well, a lot of things were lost then...other people clearing up and so forth... Anyway, I do remember that whilst I was eager to know where we were bound for, I thought Hanslip a fool for disclosing our destination, then taking the *Alert* into Bergen but stopping all shore-leave. It was bound to lead to trouble not least because while the wardroom knew our objective and had a partial grasp of the need for secrecy, the crew did not, they simply thought denial of liberty a breach of their rights. It did not help that the officers were confined to the ship too because Hanslip and Geoffrey Hardacre went ashore several times and our stay alongside Bergen's wonderful old quay became prolonged. Had it been a matter of hours, even a couple of days, we might not have stirred-up ill-feeling among the hands; as it was we lay there for several days, quite idle.

I asked Alan Tomkins why, but he only shrugged, and said all he knew was that we were awaiting 'further orders,' though what they constituted I never discovered, though Alan thought further revelations from Madame Blavatskoya were the most likely reason. One was forced to conclude that while Hardacre was filing some copy – though he had as yet little enough to work on – Hanslip was dancing to old Southmoore's tune.

It didn't seem important at the time, but we lay ten days in Bergen, eight of which were definitely bad for morale and the consumption of stores, and since we had not been at sea very long before arriving, after our departure we effectively had to go through the whole bloody shake-down procedure again so that when, on the third day out, the weather dusted up, we were not really prepared, though Alan and the Bosun had the ship herself snugged down.

Incidentally, I should say that I had at least spent a good deal of my enforced leisure reading up about navigation in Arctic waters. I won't bore you but there are a few things you need to understand in view of what happened. As you approach the North Pole the meridians of longitude converge, so that one's longitude changes rapidly. In addition one's magnetic compasses become less reliable, being subject to a downward attraction owing to your proximity to the vast mass of iron under the earth's surface that creates the magnetic field and, so to speak, breaks the surface near the poles. At the time of the year – the Arctic summer – we could expect twenty-four hours of daylight once we passed the Lofoten Islands and there was the unknown ice situation. The charts and Admiralty sailing directions showed the summer ice limit as well to the south of Kvitøya and I wondered, somewhat idly at the time, if our delay in Bergen was not to receive Madame Blavatskoya's prediction of the season's ice edge!

Having read a number of other books, all of them borrowed from Alan Tomkins and including Lord Dufferin's *Letters from High Latitudes* and James Lamont's *Yachting in the Arctic Seas*, I was beginning to convince myself that we stood little chance of reaching the White Island. When, in my capacity as the expedition's navigator, I broached the subject with Hanslip, he waved my concerns aside, told me to 'wait and see and simply lay courses off to twenty miles south of Spitsbergen's South Cape,' which naturally encouraged me to believe that I had got it right when I guessed old Blavatskoya had revealed something hidden to the rest of us.

We had a rough time in the gale despite being able to run before it for most of the time. It blew hard, more storm than gale, and winds in those seas are cold and unpleasant and exposed us to a discomfort few of us were prepared for, mentally or physically, though old Southmoore had shipped a decent amount of heavy-weather clothing aboard, I will say that for him. Nevertheless, we blew three sails out of their bolt-ropes and I remember after going aloft with my watch late one afternoon while Alan came up and took the deck that he said to me, 'You know Ned, this lot is letting a fine little barque down.'

'I'm sorry, Alan,' I replied, thinking he was admonishing me for my dilatory response in getting sail off her, 'but that last gust,' I explained, at which he interrupted. 'No, no, not you,' he said, shaking his head and wandering off to the narrow wing of the little bridge to stare up at the fore lower tops'l. He came back to me with a wan smile. 'She'll be all right now,' he assured me, taking his pipe out of his pocket and filling it. 'You get your head down for an hour before dinner…'

Somehow that enigmatic exchange summed up the feeling he and I, and I think Nat Gardner, had about the way things were going. A sort of inchoate sensation of, if not impending disaster, then something akin to it… An unease… an augury is perhaps a better way of putting it, though it is hard to define so long afterwards because I can't say it stopped me sleeping, or put me in mind of sailing with Ahab, or any such twaddle. It was just a feeling that things weren't quite right and we, certainly the three mates, would have to be extra watchful over the 'fine little barque,' for she was certainly that. Your father had spared no expense in fitting her out and whatever his faults – though it was probably your dad's open cheque book that secured it – Commander Hanslip had found him a sturdy vessel.

The gale blew itself out and gave us a couple of days of really fine weather. Naturally averse to using up our stock of coal we rolled along under full sail. the coast of Norway was visible on-and-off in the far distance until we found ourselves west of the Lofotens at which point Hanslip decided another stop was necessary. This was quite irrational and Alan Tomkins advised against it. Moreover, since this exchange took place in the chart-room, just abaft the wheel-house in which I then was, shortly before he relieved me at four o'clock one afternoon, I heard Hanslip's crisp response.

'When I require your advice, Mr Tomkins, I shall ask for it.'

I had withdrawn to the bridge-wing by the time Alan came out to relieve me looking like thunder. 'You heard that, I suppose,' he growled. I nodded. 'The man's a fucking idiot.' It was not the first time I had heard Alan swear, we all swore pretty freely, but Alan really meant it and I was a bit shaken at this very obvious dislocation between our captain and his executive officer. Such hiccups never bode well.

And in the Lofotens, where we wasted a further five days, we discovered our Commander drank. This came as a shock. You don't need me to tell you that your father's paper campaigned on a temperance/Methodist ticket aimed at a virtuous, hard-working, working and lower middle-class, literate and aspirational people who, God help them, will be those who win this bloody war – *if* we win it. Whatever the reasons for Hanslip's vice he seems to have had kept it hidden from Lord Southmoore and probably, as is most likely, it only surfaced when he was under stress. I suppose you might dig around the records and unearth his career, after all *you're* the journalist, all I can tell you is that he had been decorated for distinguished service in the Great War and while one assumes that comes with some sort of moral superiority over most of his fellows, this often has a darker shadow, a haunting, call it what you will, when events, sights, memories, smells even, can set off moments of black-dog or the blue devils – whatever you want to call them too. Hindsight suggests he may have spent time in Netley, or some other such hospital. I simply don't know, but if he did, I'm surprised your father, being a thorough-going news-hound, hadn't checked such a possibility out. Perhaps he hadn't thought it necessary.

By the time we departed from the Lofotens it was pretty obvious to us that our prolonged stay at Bergen and our unscheduled stop in the Norwegian Islands arose from Hanslip's sudden procrastination, for neither stop – and certainly the second – seemed to have any valid reason. Even the sending of Hardacre's so-called 'despatches' – another of Hasnslip's little aggrandising nouns – or John Sykes's photographs amounted to much at either stage of the voyage.

How did we first notice Hanslip's drinking? Well, looking back both Alan and I had remarked upon the stink of alcohol on his breath in Bergen. He had been ashore on 'ship's business,' with a shipping agent and the British vice-consul and I suppose we just thought he'd been obliged to imbibe some of the local aquavit because once we were back at sea he reverted to his old pompously assertive self, and maybe that was indeed the case. If so, and if he had previously been dried-out, the aquavit, or whatever it was, had triggered a renewal of his desire for alcohol and thinking back to his decision to put in at Reine, at the southern tip of the Lofotens, it was precipitate.

After Alan had relieved me that afternoon and was hauling the barque round onto her new heading I had gone into the chartroom to lay off the new course and initial the log-slate for my watch – Alan, as Chief Officer wrote the fair-copy daily, which was signed by Hanslip and himself, we officers-of-the-watch maintaining a running slate – I went to report to Hanslip.

He had shut his cabin door and I knocked. It took a moment for him to shout 'come in' and almost automatically I said: 'Mr Tomkins tells me we are putting into Reine, sir. I have laid off the courses,' I think I handed him or told him the ETA – the estimated time of arrival - and asked, 'would you like me to ask Sparks to signal for a pilot?'

He seemed confused by my question and it was only then that I noticed his face. Our cabins were quite small; even the Commander's, despite its position under the wheel-house, was not large and none of them were brilliantly lit. For this reason most of us, mates, engineers, sparks and our specialists, spent our time round the ward-room table under a large sky-light. I had caught a glimpse of Hanslip a few moments earlier when he had first come onto the bridge and I had retreated onto the bridge-wing. As he always had been up to then, he had been properly dressed, shirt, collar and tie, his number-two reefer jacket – every inch what he purported to be, a Commander in the Royal Naval Reserve. But within minutes of going below, collar and tie had been torn off – I remember they lay on his settee – and his shirt was open-necked, the brass collar-stud reflecting what light there was as his Adam's apple bobbed up and down below a face that looked as though he was either on the verge of tears or had actually been crying, for his eyes were blood-shot and watery and he held a crumpled handkerchief which he waved at me with a curt 'Yes, yes, of course, Two-Oh,' dismissing me smartly, coming forward and closing the door on me.

One can teeter on the verge of alcoholism oneself without the sight of a real alcoholic who's fallen over the edge filling you with a sense of disgust. I don't know why Hanslip had become one, or what he had suffered during the last war, or even if the war was responsible. Who knows? But something had robbed Hanslip of his innocence and he had found nothing to replace it. As for your father's employing him, if he was aware of Hanslip's problem, perhaps Lord Southmoore wanted to pick-up a reformed alcoholic and give him back his self-respect and self-esteem.

To reiterate, I can see now why he, Hanslip that is, had employed Alan Tomkins, Nat Gardner and myself as his deck officers. We were, as it were, no threat to him. As I said before, Tomkins's solid expertise was vital while Nat and I, both coming from a back-ground familiar to Hanslip, were the right sort of boys, so to speak, whereas had he employed the Arctic experts, the old whaling and sealing men that sat hopefully in the Fleet Street waiting room, he would have felt inadequate from the word go. As it was it was only as we approached the Arctic Circle that Hanslip realised what he had let himself in for and I think it was this that triggered his drinking. I'm sure he left London fully dried-out, but there was gin, scotch and beer in the mess, and he saw us enjoying our daily tot or two in a cheerfully carefree way. It is what one did at sea, a small compensation for the things we gave up by following our curious calling. But he found it intolerable; my guess is our stop at Blyth unsettled him while the prolonged sojourn at Bergen did the real damage. However, we might have avoided all that followed had we not steamed into Reine.

I wasn't on the bridge when the pilot boarded, being called for stand-by shortly before we arrived off the berth, but Nat, who was, told me that when the pilot asked, Hanslip told him we had come in for some repairs. What these were was a mystery, for Owen Jones's engines were running smoothly, we had used very little coal since leaving Blyth, and that mainly in the galley stove, while the only damage we had suffered was aloft, when we blew out those three sails. Being the good man he was and having a Bosun as good as *he* was – I wish I could remember his name – Alan Tomkins had had the remains of the wrecked sails sent down and new ones sent aloft and bent on the instant the weather moderated. Nat, being the decent chap he was, thought Hanslip was just being cagey and that the change of plan was due to some reason connected with Southmoore's secret mission. It had bizarre enough foundations to lend credibility to this hypothesis, but as the barque lay idle alongside with Hanslip off ashore and the officers and specialists – let's call them the wardroom gang – milling about for a pre-dinner noggin at noon, it was clear this was unlikely because it was Hardacre that was the first to voice his misgivings.

A newspaper-man not used to the kind of restraints we seafarers felt, he stared round us with his bullish glare and almost demanded Alan Tomkins tell us what the hell we were doing in port again. Without waiting for a reply he turned on poor Owen Jones, virtually accusing him of the incompetent running of the engine-room department, whereupon Jones read him his fortune.

'There's nothing wrong with my engines, nor my boilers, steering gear, auxies, pumps or anything under the fiddley, damn you. Keep your fucking' – excuse the language, but it conveys much of the mood of those using it – 'nose out of what doesn't concern you and if you write a word of slander to that effect, Boy-oh, I'll have your guts for garters.'

Used to rebuffs, Hardacre swung round on Alan. 'Well, Number One,' he asked sarcastically. 'Perhaps *you* can tell us…'

Alan, who was already onto Hanslip's sudden drinking, shrugged loyally. 'I guess Commander Hanslip has his reasons,' he said mildly.

'You bet he has,' retorted Hardacre, thereby hinting that he knew more than he was saying.

'Well perhaps you can tell us then,' snapped Jones, 'instead of playing your cocky London games with us.'

Hardacre stared round the wardroom at us all. I could see the effect his raking glance had on our scientists; they were distinctly uncomfortable. Nat and I might have been public school boys in the widest sense of the expression, but our three boffins were hot-housed, graduates, not at all used to disruption which wasn't of their own self-indulgent making. I sensed them rather frightened of Hardacre who certainly lived up to his apt surname. Interestingly John Sykes, though standing next to him as though in support, seemed less of a threat, but the outcome of this relatively mild little upset was that Maddox, Cronshaw and Doughty withdrew to their self-styled 'lab,' Owen Jones took John Rayne off to his beloved engines and Sparks announced that he would take advantage of not being required in his radio shack to write home. 'I suppose I'll be allowed to post a letter,' he remarked rather plaintively as he departed for his caboose.

That left us three mates and Crichton, the Doctor. 'Well, Doc?' Alan asked relaxing and taking his pipe out of his pocket, 'Any theories?'

Crichton, a man much older than the rest of us and one of very few words, who seemed to exist entirely inside his head, and that was generally in a book, sighed and lifted one hand from its place on the ward-room table beside a gin-and-water, then dropped it with a faint thump. 'You should know better than to ask a physician…'

'So he *is* your patient,' broke in Nat, sharp as ever, 'you know there's a reason behind our good Commander's conduct.

'I didn't say that, young man,' Crichton responded coolly. 'All I know is that the ship is alongside in port and the prospect of it being so is scarcely alluring…'

At this point the steward entered and asked if he could lay the table for lunch, whereupon Alan said quickly to Nat and me, 'you two, the chart-room, bring your drinks.'

We scrambled after him and gathered in the empty chart-room from where we had a commanding view of the quay and gangway. When we had perched ourselves on the chart-room settee with Alan leaning on the chart-table, half turned towards us he said:

'Closet drinker, I suspect. I also suspect Crichton and Hardacre know something about our gallant Captain, all of which makes our position invidious...mine in particular, as I am sure you are both sufficiently experienced to appreciate.'

'Appreciate it, yes, but...' Nat said hesitantly.

Neither of us had actually been in such a situation where a Master's authority might require challenge and I heard Alan Tomkins sigh. He smiled wanly and looked from Nat Gardner to me.

'Well no, I understand.' He looked ashore where a road led uphill, away from the small quay among the brightly painted houses and buildings that, for barely a quarter of a mile, constituted Reine. It had begun to – appropriately enough – rain, as it did so often on the Norwegian coast and I think he expected to be caught by Hanslip plotting his downfall, but the two or three stalwart Scowegians in the street just turned up their collars and plodded on, about their business; of Herbert Henry there was no sign. The place was essentially a fishing port, so where Hanslip was, we could only guess. Tomkins turned back to us.

'Well, we will just have to carry-on as though everything's fine and dandy, but I will say one thing, we must all three of us be extra vigilant that the ship is not endangered. If our voyage is prolonged, I shan't complain, for any employment is better than nothing, but I'm damned if I am losing my ticket and you two would do well to think about your own.' He paused to let the words sink in, adding, 'I can smell a decent meal, let's go and eat.'

By some tacit telepathy Nat and I let him go, clattering down the chart-room stairs back into the saloon from whence arose the aroma of pea-soup.

'What d'you think?' Nat asked me, as if I had any better idea than he did. 'Is this as big a bugger's muddle as he suggests?'

I considered the question a moment. 'Lush or not, the Old Man was sober when he joined the ship, which suggests that he did not join with a vast quantity of booze and had every intention of behaving himself. If he got booze in Blyth or Bergen he must have run out of it. As long as we weather the interim, maybe he won't be a problem once we get into the High Arctic.'

'The High Arctic,' Nat repeated in his booming voice and with a grin large enough to match as he turned away and followed Tomkins down into the saloon. 'That's very poetic, Ned,' he added as he drew out his chair and took his seat at the ward-room table. Tomkins was already tucking-in his napkin and Owen Jones had just finished the soup. 'But,' Nat went on, having ordered soup, 'have any of us actually been there?'

'Where's that boyo?' the Chief Engineer enquired.

'The High Arctic,' boomed Nat.

'Bin in the Antarctic, whaling,' said Owen Jones, shortly. 'Lot of ice,' he said simply. 'Made a nice warm engine-room the only place to be. I suspect the High Arctic is much the same.'

We laughed and then Alan said quietly, 'I've been north; Labrador, the Davis Straits, sealing out of Newfie, St John… As the Chief says, lots of ice.'

'And penguins,' added Jones.

'No, no penguins in the north,' said Tomkins. 'Polar bears. No polar bears in the Antarctic.'

'Well,' said the Chief genially and somewhat consequentially, 'you pays your money and you takes your choice.' He lifted his napkin to his lips and belched discreetly before staring at the Chief Officer across the table. 'When's the Old Man going to rejoin us and give us some sailing orders then, Alan?'

'In his own good time, I imagine, Chief.'

'Well,' replied Jones, digging into the meat pie the steward had just set down before him, 'then I think that I'll get some shut-eye on the old settee this afternoon… What are you young buggers laughing at?'

'Well, isn't that what you always do, Chief, Old Man or not,' said Nat Gardner with a wide grin.

'You should teach your young colleagues some respect, Mister Mate,' Jones said with mock severity, dabbing his lips, 'we can't have oil and water riling each other on a ship this small.'

'Well, that's true, Chief,' replied Tomkins, pouring himself a glass of water and turning to regard Nat and I who were both still amused by the Chief's desire to explain away his quotidian habits. 'You mind your manners my young friends,' Tomkins said, good-naturedly. 'Ah, here's the Doc….'

Crichton entered the saloon and took his place. 'Now, see, boys,' said Jones, 'here's another busy man.'

Crichton looked round the table and gave his thin-lipped smile. 'I am your insurance policy, gentlemen, and like all insurance policies, am not obliged to do anything until something goes awry.'

'Well, I hope you remain a gentleman of leisure for the whole voyage,' put in the journalist Hardacre, catching the mood of gentle banter. 'Can't say I'm much overworked at the moment either. What about you lot?' he asked the three scientists.

'We take our readings and record our data,' answered Cronshaw the geologist, 'but I must confess being stuck here isn't exactly what I expected. Anyway, where *is* the Captain?'

It was, of course, the question the professional seafarers amongst us had been avoiding and only a somewhat naive outsider could have asked in that situation, in front of the steward.

'Ashore on ship's business,' answered Tomkins shortly.

Prompting Owen Jones, who was by then well into the spotted-dick, to add bluntly, 'so mind your own.'

'Sorry,' responded Cronshaw, mightily offended.

'Forget it,' said Tomkins with an air of finality which ended the brittle mood. As far as I can remember no-one said anything else until, for some reason, Nat and I found ourselves back on the bridge, yarning.

'Well, now we know why Alan got the job of Mate,' He remarked, his voice unusually quiet. Clearly he was of the same mind as myself.

'Yes,' I replied, my opinion of the Chief Officer rising by the day.

'I reckon he's scared,' Nat said after a moment's silence.

'Who Hanslip?'

'Yes, sorry. I don't think much scares Mr Tomkins.'

'No, nor do I.'

'He's either frightened of the job of command – lost his nerve as so many blokes did after the war, or there's some more personal reason.'

I shrugged. 'In my experience you don't need an excuse or a reason for turning alcoholic. It's my theory that some personalities have a predisposition to become a lush.'

'I dislike that word.'

'What, "lush"?'

'Uh, huh. It's a euphemism and fails to carry weight. "Drunk," "sot," are all much better.' He paused, then said: 'Hey, maybe it has something to do with his being up north during the Allied Intervention.'

'Oh, I don't know,' I said yawning. 'Nor do I care much as to why, just having him in charge is going to be more of a problem than Alan is prepared to admit just at the moment.'

'He's pretty worried about it, I think.' I agreed and Nat

suppressed a belch. 'Christ, that plum duff certainly makes good settee ballast. Maybe the Chief's got the right idea… There's nothing else to do, is there?'

I remember looking round the wheelhouse, then walking into the chart-room where all my charts were in as good an order as the paucity of instructions permitted, before coming back into the wheelhouse. 'No, let's get some shut-eye ourselves.'

'D'you think the Mate'll mind…'

'Why don't you ask him?' said Alan from the bottom of the companionway with a smile, puffing on his pipe so that he looked up through a wreath of aromatic blue smoke, his face caught in a shaft of sunlight coming through the companionway skylight. Funny, I shall always remember him like that: quiet, confident, every inch the professional sea-officer…a great guy in his unassuming way…

'Stop nattering like women round the parish-pump and get your heads down for an hour if you're sure there is nothing else demanding your attention.'

I, no, we, were woken two hours later by a great bellow. Thinking something was seriously wrong all of us who had retreated into our cabins for a post-prandial snooze appeared in our cabin doorways to be treated to the sight of Commander Hanslip DSC RNR descending the companionway under the influence of alcohol and gravity, and certainly not his own legs, for he fell into a heap at the bottom, his black tie awry, his hat by his side and his face florid with anger. It was a farcical sight actually, though it was immediately clear no good would come of it.

Tomkins attempted to pretend Hanslip had – forgive the pun - slipped on the steps of the companionway. Indeed the wretched man made some comment about them being slippery before shrugging off the Chief Officer's proffered hand and getting to his feet. He found it necessary to support his dignity by holding onto the nearest chair back at the mess-table before looking round at us.

‘Is this what you do when I am absent on the ship’s affairs? Where was the officer of the deck? I was received by no-one at the gangway, no-one at all…’ his voice increased in vigour and conviction as he went on in similar vein for some moments, berating us all for our general slackness and incompetence, telling us that in an earlier age he would have had us all cobbed, or flogged, or mast-headed, or some other such ridiculous nonsense until he simply ran out of steam, whereupon Alan Tomkins put his oar in.

‘I apologise if the quartermaster was not on the gangway to greet you, sir,’ he said reasonably, ‘but as things are very quiet here and I thought there was no danger of unwanted visitors, I have had him checking some stores with the boatswain. As for the officers, Commander Hanslip, they had my permission to relax as I was up and about, though I was in my cabin working.’

‘You’re a fucking liar, Mister,’ Hanslip said unpleasantly, slurring his speech.

‘I think you ought to turn-in yourself, sir,’ Alan responded coolly.

‘Turn-in? Turn-in? Whatever for, the ship’s sailing in half an hour. The pilot will be here soon. What d’you think I have been doing ashore?’

‘I wasn’t aware that it took four days to arrange a pilot, even in a dead-and-alive place like this and I still suggest that you turn-in. We’ll see the ship safely to sea…’

‘The devil you will, Mister. She’s my ship and my responsibility…’ He lugged at his pocket watch, appeared to have some difficulty reading it and then said, ‘pipe the men to stations for leaving harbour in ten minutes.’

‘I think that I had better check they are all on board first, sir, if you don’t mind.’

'What?' roared Hanslip, 'I didn't give permission for any shore-leave…'

'No, but in your absence, I did,' Alan said quietly. I knew he was making a point and that he had ensured no-one was ashore at eight o'clock that morning when he had all hands out to wash down the decks and then clean paintwork, but, of course, Hanslip saw this as just one more chip at his own authority. 'Mr Manners went to leave some mail for the *Hurtigruten*,' he explained, 'I'll see if he is back on board.'

Hanslip stood swaying and babbling about not having two men in command while we took our cue from Alan and went about our business for going to sea. On the one hand we were grateful for something positive to do; on the other we feared the consequences of going to sea with a drunken master on the bridge.

'Oh ho,' Nat stage-whispered into me ear, 'I thought it was the crew who were supposed to be the devil in harbour, isn't that what old Admiral Napier said?'

'I don't know what old Admiral Napier said,' I remember responding, 'but I think we are going to leave a wonderful impression of Britannia's rule in Reine…'

We dispersed to our stations and I heard Tomkins blow his whistle for the hands to muster. A moment later, as I reached the *Alert*'s little poop-deck, I watched the pilot run up the gangway. It was the same man that had guided us into Reine and a few moments later I was involved with singling-up, watching the hands coil down the after mooring ropes, lift the fenders inboard as soon as we were clear of the quay and Owen Jones's Singer sewing machine was trundling away under my feet. We swung away and headed north-east, through the Leads inside the Lofotens. Half-an-hour later the pilot had been discharged and we were on our own. Having checked everything was secure aft of the low centre-castle which, incidentally, provided the officers and some of the crew with their accommodation, I made my way up to the bridge. As Third Officer, Nat's station was on the bridge and seeing me he nodded his head at Hanslip who was fast asleep in the one chair allowed in the tiny wheelhouse.

'Been like that since the pilot boarded.'

'What was the pilot's reaction?' I remember asking, ashamed of our Commander's conduct. Nat laughed. 'I told him that our captain had had a very bad war, that he would be fine once we were at sea…'

'That was resourceful of you,' I said.

' "They drink a lot here," the pilot said, "I expect he spent too much time with the chandler," ' Nat recounted with a chuckle, adding, 'so the national honour was just about saved.'

'Ah,' I half-jested, 'the *Worcester* training will out.'

*

Hanslip disappeared into his cabin and reappeared next morning as though nothing out-of-the-ordinary had happened. Perhaps in his imagination nothing had. Anyway, we steamed clear of the Lofotens, shut Owen Jones's iron-ware down and hoisted sail. I was beginning to enjoy conning the ship under sail and, to be truthful, despite the shenanigans in Reine, this passage proved to be the happiest of the entire voyage. The weather improved as we sailed north under all sail, a steady moderate breeze blowing out of the north-east had us close hauled and while the air was cold, coming as it did from a northerly quarter, and we were close-hauled on the starboard tack, I do remember it was surprisingly warm out of the breeze in brilliant sunshine, the sea was a deep blue and we carried all plain sail, bowling along at a creditable rate of knots.

The only thing that sort-of marred what would otherwise have been an unsullied delight, was the appearance of Hanslip on the bridge at midnight, oh, I suppose on the second night out from

Reine… No, maybe the third; anyway, we were well clear of the land. I had come up in the bridge to relieve Nat and, as was customary I went first into the chart-room where I expected to find the Night Order Book signed by the Old Man. It was laid out on the chart, but not written in for that night, so having made myself a mug of tea from the pot prepared at the after part of the chart-room, I went out onto the bridge-wing and found Nat leaning on the rail behind the canvas dodger with Hanslip beside him.

'Ahh, good morning Ned,' Nat boomed, straitening-up as I approached. Hanslip looked round but did not otherwise acknowledge my presence. I recall looking up at the sails lit-up by the midnight sun which glowed low on the northern horizon as Nat handed over to me, course to steer and what-not. With the Commander on the bridge he was almost pompously formal and, briefly, turning round to see that Hanslip had resumed staring forward again, made a curious little gesture with his thumb, towards Hanslip, simultaneously pulling a face which I instinctively interpreted as distaste, or disgust, or something of the sort.

Without lingering for our usual chat Nat dropped his voice, murmured 'Good luck' and then, raising it, said, 'I've handed over to the Second Officer, sir and bid you good night.'

Given that our usual partings at this hour were of a less than polite nature, I realised Nat was putting me on my guard, so I said 'Good morning, sir,' and walked out to the extremity of the bridge-wing with my mug of tea and looked about me, as though taking stock – which in fact I was, and usually did once I had the con. Apart from my 'good morning' I did not deliberately ignore Hanslip's presence, but it was not my place to cosy up to him and adopt the same position as that in which I had found Nat and I guessed that it had not been of his choosing either.

Anyway, I was just about to cross the bridge and do the same thing on the port side when Hanslip called me over. 'Two-Oh.'

'Sir?'

He patted the thick teak cap-rail that ran round the bridge, indicating that I should now take Nat's station beside him. 'I was just saying to the Third Officer,' he began, 'that we must begin to keep a sharp lookout for old ice. This wind may bring some growlers down from the ice-edge and we should be on the lookout for them.'

From my reading of the Sailing Directions, I knew what a growler was, an old piece of ice that floated barely clear of the water but which could be quite large. Moreover, I thought Hanslip's remark about meeting them a little premature but contented myself with an 'aye, aye, sir,' and lest this should sound too abrupt, added, 'lovely night.'

'Yes,' Hanslip agreed, whereupon an awkward silence fell upon us. Rather gauchely I tried my best.

'I'm looking forward to getting a bit further north, never having been this far before. We used to have ice a-plenty in the Gulf of Po Hai, to be sure, but that was considerably further south than we are now.'

'Yes,' Hanslip said again. It was clear that he was winding himself up to say something. After a bit it came out. He coughed and picked up my earlier remark. 'Yes, it is a lovely night. Good to be at sea,' he added with a touch of pomposity before saying, 'much better to be at sea than in port. I was decidedly unwell in Reine. Had a drink with the agent and it turned my guts. Laid me up sick for several days. Good to have reliable officers who kept the show on the road. Most grateful…' His voice trailed off, he straightened up, slapped the rail and said in a suddenly decisive tone of voice as though his conduct in the Lofotens was all explained, justified, done-and-dusted, 'right, well give me five minutes to write up the night's orders and then come and sign them.'

And that was that. I did as I was bid, counter-signed his orders to show that I read and understood them and then with a curt 'good night,' he disappeared below to his pit.

The whole little episode had taken no more than fifteen to twenty minutes but it left me and, I learned later, Nat Gardner feeling distinctly iffy about Commander Herbert Henry Hanslip, Royal Naval Reserve, and his powers of self-deception.

*

It's getting late but I only have three more evenings to tell the rest of the story and if you want to hear more tonight, I think you should. I don't think I have wasted your time because without the preamble the finale won't make a great deal of sense and it will certainly not satisfy your father.

Okay? Good.

We continued our passage north and east, tacking for the greater part of the way as the wind veered and backed a bit, then and settled again in the north-east, all of which lost us a good deal of time, but Hanslip had suddenly become conscious not merely that the days were slipping by, but to rely upon our steam-engine would consume more coal. The wind now remained steady from the north-east, give or take a point or two, so we beat our way up wind passing Bear Island which we closed to about five miles before old Herbert Henry got a cold funk and we put about. One thing I will say about it though, was that it was fine sailing and Alan Tomkins was in his element. Nat and I learned a great deal of the finer – and now completely arcane – points about trimming sails to get the best out of a square-rigged vessel going to windward. Whether it was by sheer chance, or cunning design, your old dad really had bought a rather fine little barque, but I'm repeating myself, nevertheless, for one bred to steam I found myself reluctantly admiring the capabilities of a well-handled sailing vessel which ran counter to all the orthodoxy of my professional training in the Blue Funnel Line.

We didn't see the South Cape of Spitsbergen but soon ran into the ice, I forget where or when but I suppose it was somewhere south-east of Edge Island. It was loose pack, pushed down from the north through the Hindlopen Strait and we still had I suppose about sixty miles to run to reach the White Island. The weather remained mild for our latitude, which was seventy something north and we were miles from the starting point of Andrée's balloon ride which was away on the far north-western edge of the Svalbard Archipelago at what had once been a whaling base fort the Dutch in the seventeenth century, a place they called rather colourfully Smeerenberg, though it was in fact no more than an anchorage. Here they – the Swedes that is - had mixed iron filings and hydrochloric acid to make hydrogen to fill their ill-fated balloon before lighting off for the pole, full of expectation and dreams.

Looking back, we were not so very different; the closer we got to the White Island, the more those of us in 'the know' dwelt upon Madame Blavatskoya's clairvoyance. I'm not certain even now what I thought about it at this time, but as a sceptic I don't think I thought much beyond the fact that the expedition offered me a great opportunity for an experience that might prove valuable and, as Alan Tomkins repeatedly pointed-out, provided employment.

Whatever our private thoughts, whatever the irrational conduct of Herbert Henry and whatever the reliability that could be placed upon Blavatskoya, we were a fine little ship and our crew had, despite the conduct of their Commander, settled down under Alan's and the Bosun's close eyes as we started our assault on the ice.

This began with a ward-room discussion which turned upon at which point did we fire-up the boilers, lower the screw – oh, did I tell you that for sailing and protecting it if we were caught fast in the ice, you could disconnect it from the drive-shaft and lift it into the hull? No? I thought that I had. Anyway, it was a cunning bit of kit, designed originally, I think, for the Victorian navy where, in the days of auxiliary steam frigates, when they changed from steam to sail, they could lift the screw out of the water to prevent it dragging and slowing the ship. It rotated in what was called a banjo-frame – don't ask me why – but this could be lifted into a well in the ship's counter. One had to be careful to get the shaft and the screw realigned when you next wanted to use it but that was essentially an engineering problem.

Anyway, though conscious that his coal stocks were finite, Owen Jones was both eager to use his steam engine and confident that we carried a pretty generous supply. As bags of the stuff seemed to be everywhere and the bunkers were filled to over-flowing, no-one gave the matter a great deal of serious consideration at this time. If Blavatskoya was correct, all we had to do was reach the island, locate the wreckage of the Swedes' balloon, take the photos and come home. Put like this it all seems pretty bizarre now, but that is how it seemed to us then. Either that, or we found nothing where Blavatskoya said we would and we all came home anyway with the boffins having gathered some data. This was before the Kylsant scandal and the Great Depression and we did not question the decisions of great – and by that I chiefly mean rich – men and their whims. We were born to servitude whether we were the grubby products of Cardiff's Tiger Bay toiling in the engine-room, or the polished products of the *Conway* and *Worcester*, like Nat and I. You've got to remember that while Mussolini was already making a name for himself, no-one in Britain took him seriously and no-body had heard of Herr Hitler.

Sorry, I digress and am wasting time, but the nub of the day's discussion revolved around Hanslip and Owen's desire to flash-up the boilers and get the ship under steam and my calculations of distance. We weren't making any headway under sail and that afternoon, although we had – by some miracle – found a lead, a channel of open water, what the Russians call a *polynya* and it led in roughly the right direction, we could not expect it to go on for many more miles and, sure enough, it failed before the day was out. Owen Jones got his way, and we began shoving our way through increasingly thick ice under steam.

I can't really recall much detail of the next week or two. For the Arctic, the weather remained relatively benign; lots of low fog and by-and-large a fluky wind from the north-east, all of which gave us a good deal of trouble making progress towards Kvitøya through the ice. Watches became tedious re-runs of the previous day, then the previous week as we found a lead, steamed or sailed down it, only to find that while we might have made five miles progress, we then had to cast about for some new opportunity.

We did have, I recall, a few days delay while another gale came through and the ice closed in on us. It blew like hell, the little ice spicules hitting us like small bird-shot as the *Alert* rolled and ground against the ice. The temperature dropped and Hanslip did his impression of Shackleton by trying to force the vessel through the ice until the Chief mentioned the daily consumption of coal, at which point he desisted. Eventually, of course, the depression moved through and things calmed down again.

During all this Hanslip fretted mightily, coming up on the bridge at irregular intervals, taking command when we found a bit of a lead then going below again when the ice shut-in. He muttered a lot to himself and his comments to us, the Mates, seemed increasingly odd, strangely disconnected with the matter-in-hand, though to be truthful, he didn't say a great deal to either Nat or myself, though I knew that he talked a good deal to Alan Tomkins.

I got the distinct impression that he thought the difficulties of finding a way through the ice was a personal insult offered him by an implacable fate, for he regularly lost his temper when the lead shut in, proving to be the most impatient of men. The rest of us found it rather a challenge, I think.

Most of the ice was old pack, interspersed with small bergs, but occasionally we'd find a large berg stuck in the ice-field, wonderfully spiky things, some of them, with fantastical profiles – nothing like the pictures of bergs you see in books about Scott's or Shackleton's Antarctic adventures. Up in the Artic, 'under the bear,' it's very different to the *Ant*arctic but we didn't take much notice of the aesthetic merit of our surroundings; the ice had just become an enemy. It would have been *the* enemy had the process of our disintegration not begun, but it was, I think, the ice that triggered it.

Unfortunately it began with that mildest of men, Owen Jones, who at dinner one day mentioned to a pretty full ward-room – Nat was on watch – about the inroads all the faffing about was making into our coal reserves. We all knew this and certainly among the deck officers it had been an underlying feature of our general concerns, mentioned when handing over the watch, and so forth. Although we had been using the sails whenever we could, you can't shut-down the boilers when you might need them again so that even when not under power, you are still using a certain amount of coal. We knew too that the Chief made a daily report to Hanslip on fuel, just as Tomkins did on water, but Hanslip, who had just taken his place at the head of the wardroom table, took exception.

'This is not the place to be mentioning coal stocks,' he upbraided Owen Jones.

Jones looked up astonished. 'I'm sorry, sir, I just thought…'

'Well stop bloody well thinking,' snapped Hanslip, taking up his soup spoon. Amongst most of us this would have precluded any further remark, but good old Jonesy was, in his own way, as touchy about rank as Hanslip and regarded the rank of chief engineer as a senior one. Certainly, as Alan Tomkins explained it to me afterwards, he was not used to being publicly humiliated, and his Welsh blood was up, so-to-speak. He made a *sotto voce* comment.

'*What* did you say?' said a flushing and soup-spluttering Hanslip.

Quite unabashed, the Chief replied, 'I said that won't do us any good, will it?' I can quite clearly recall the strong Welsh lilt to his voice, because he went on to press his point with a certain amount of license. 'You don't want a chief engineer who *doesn't think*, Captain, do you? *You think* about that, Boy-O; not up here in all this bloody ice.' He used to say 'ploody ice'.

Well that was it for Hanslip: the answering-back and the 'Boy-O,' unintentional or not, absolutely *infuriated* him.

'You mind your damned manners, Jones,' he snarled, his face beetroot-red as he made a passing attempt to control his temper but I could see quite clearly that it wasn't just what Hanslip thought of as insubordination that triggered the outburst, but something else. He went on to deliver himself of a rant about 'respect for rank' and the importance of the 'maintenance of proper discipline and order, particularly in difficult circumstances,' all of which was supposed to put a gloss on the affair, but it merely made Jones lay down his knife and fork and rise from the table.

'Where are you going, Jones? I'm talking to you…'

'You're talking *at* me, Captain, and I've had all I want to eat, so,' and here he looked round at the rest of us, quite unfazed by Hanslip's behaviour and said, 'excuse me gentlemen.'

Of course, those of us who knew the Chief knew his politeness, but I think Hanslip thought the allusion to 'gentlemen' excluded him. It was all quite ridiculous, but he threw down his cutlery and stalked out of the wardroom. Thereafter he reverted to the naval formality of eating alone in his cabin, which increased the poor steward's burden, though it left the rest of us a degree of freedom, best expressed by Second Engineer Rayne who subsequently remarked that mealtimes had improved 'now that the bear ate in his lair'.

You are probably thinking all this very puerile, and it was in its way, but aboard ships such stupid rows, caused by collisions of cultures, or incipient mental break-down, can take on an impetus and character of their own. Old Jonesy might have blown-up in true Celtic fashion, but he didn't, to his credit, though I think he went below to his beloved engines and did some entirely unnecessary overhauling until he had worked his ire out of his system.

Anyway, I went on the bridge to relieve Nat and was in the throes of rendering a quiet and rapid account of the incident when Alan came on the bridge.

'Get your dinner,' he said abruptly to Nat before turning to me and indicating we should go out onto the bridge-wing.

'You know what that was all about, don't you?' he said, his face betraying a deep anxiety.

'Well I suppose…' I began but Alan's query was purely rhetorical.

He gestured round him. 'It's this ice; it compounds the delay he caused by his adventures in Bergen and Reine. The bloody man's quite unstable and incapable of command. Now he has no sauce to fall back on, or if he has, he hasn't taken anything yet.' Alan let the sentence hang ominously before going on to say: 'My guess is the next few hours will tell us whether he has a secret store or not. Either way it's going to be rocky, so don't you let him catch you gossiping with the Third Mate like that.'

I felt truly chastened. The subject of Hanslip and his erratic behaviour had become such an important feature of our life on board in the last few days, as we laboured painfully north-east through the pack-ice, that I hadn't regarded my quick briefing to Nat as anything other than a recounting of the ship's gossip. Alan's cautionary remark told me that he was trying to manage a seriously deteriorating situation, so I apologised.

'Don't worry,' he said, 'I just don't want you two to be giving him any pretexts for doing something stupid. Actually he thinks the world of you both. Jones didn't know what he was doing and that was all most unfortunate.'

I remember having a sort of flash of intuition, though I think that I had half-guessed the fact from having seen Alan and Dr Crichton having a chat on deck a few days earlier. The Doc didn't go on deck much, preferring his cabin and the company of a book, and without really thinking it through, I clocked the fact that the two of them had come on deck to speak privately in what looked like a purely casual chat as they stared out over the ice.

'You've been talking to the Doc,' I ventured, 'and he knows something.'

Alan gave me a sharp look. 'You're perceptive…' I explained. 'Oh, yes, well, you're quite right,' Alan went on. 'Not that he confided much but apparently he'd dried Hanslip out after the war and when Hanslip got the appointment to command the *Alert* from your father he must have had second thoughts, because he looked Crichton up, told him where he was going and when Crichton asked if a quack had been appointed to the ship and was told no, advised Hanslip to go back to your father and suggest that one was added to the complement, telling your father that he knew someone who would be able to drop his practice and volunteer 'out of a love of adventure'. This was pure bullshit, of course. Crichton's retired, and quite well-off. So he's come along for the benefit of one pathetic alkie, so, now we know…'

A thought struck me and I remarked, 'he wasn't at the dinner table.'

'No, he wasn't. He was sitting in his cabin and stayed there until the row with Jones had blown over. I popped in to see him after you had come up here to relieve Nat. He said he wanted to hear how Hanslip handled the affair…'

'Handled it?' I remember saying. 'He started it.'

'Yes, yes, but you know what I mean…'

'What? Keeping the patient under observation?'

'Something like that. It's my guess that Crichton's presence is what's keeping our gallant Commander from completely losing control.' Alan paused a moment, then asked, 'you haven't seen them together, hugger-mugger, or anything like that?'

'No, but they could speak confidentially at any time.' I recall musing a moment, then adding the comment that Crichton made no effort to stop Hanslip going on the toot in Reine.

Alan shook his head. 'I mentioned that and Crichton said that he had been reading in his cabin when the Old Man slipped ashore, so had no chance to stop him. Anyway,' he concluded, 'I don't want to be seen talking to you like this, so I'm going to bugger off and catch some shut-eye before eight-bells.'

Tomkins left me to stare out over the ice. We were on half-speed, pushing ourselves through some thin ice and making quite good progress, but in the next hour or so things changed. I had to do some backing-and-filling, going ahead and astern, to get anywhere at all. It all used up coal.

Shall we call it a day? You're yawning and I am growing boring.

THE THIRD EVENING - THE WHITE ISLAND

Before we go on I want to say something about Hanslip. I really don't want to give the impression that we were sailing under a latter-day Captain Bligh. You journalists turn easily to commonly comprehended references and clichés, but Hanslip was no William Bligh. Besides being excessively bad-tempered, Bligh was a supremely competent seaman who, even standing amid the wreckage of his career, never took to drink though his bad-language was legendary.

Hanslip, on the other hand, was a grievously wounded man and, God knows, this present war is creating a lot of them, particularly at sea where no-one sees what we endure and we lack the glamour of the Brylcream Boys of the RAF. The Crabs might have saved Britain from a German invasion, though they would have proved totally ineffective if Gerry had actually got afloat and made the effort to cross the Channel, but it's out there, in the Western Ocean that Britain is being saved – if she is, and I'm by no means convinced of this for all the effort, blood, sweat, tears and treasure that are being expended by our little island…

Sorry, I digress, I merely wish to make the point that I can now better recognise what was happening to Hanslip, a personal insight that was denied me all those years ago aboard the *Alert* as she struggled through the pack-ice. Alan Tomkins knew, so too did Doc Crichton, for Crichton, perceiving how the land lay, partially broke his Hippocratic oath to the extent of warning Alan that circumstances might arise in which he had to take over the ship. It was a pity your father didn't know. Somehow Hanslip had wormed his way so far into your dad's good books that Lord Southmoore saw only what he wanted to see. Perhaps Crichton thought he had cured Hanslip, perhaps your father thought he had, but in retrospect the late appointment of a doctor to the ship was, of course, significant. Anyway…

It took us, oh, I really can't recall how many days to reach Kvitøya. It's some miles to the east of North-East Land, the unromantically named large island that lies east of West Spitsbergen. It's low – Kvitøya I mean - and by the time we got there it was around the end of May, I think. It was a good month before mid-summer and still the weather held, just the occasional drifting fog and sea-smoke, but nothing to worry us beyond the pressures of the pack-ice fields and the steadily diminishing stock of coal. Not then, anyway. I think we were to some extent lulled into a false sense of security, coping well with the ice, while no-one dared mention the coal again, at least not publically. It seemed that if Hanslip was worried about being in the ice, as Alan Tomkins surmised, then most of his anxieties were of his own making.

Still, as I was saying, Kvitøya is low-lying. These islands, being of dark rock heat-up in the sun and you often find there is clear water close to the shore, so that you can anchor safely. At that time of the year there was twenty-four hour daylight and, had we not been keeping watches, one could lose track of the time of day.

I think that we were all pretty excited to have reached our destination. Hanslip certainly was; it was relief, I suppose, but he was like a school-boy let out for the summer holidays. He was all for going ashore directly and starting to search the island, a plan that immediately appealed to Hardacre and Sykes who were, I think, bored out of their skulls and were eager to get their 'story,' if there was one to get. Our three scientists were equally keen to set-up a 'shore observatory,' though to what end I was never quite sure. It's all a bit woolly now; they had been collecting data since we left Blyth. I'm afraid I cannot remember all the details, though I think one of them produced a rather well regarded paper after it was all over and it was this that 'justified' the expedition in the event. I was away to sea almost immediately on my return, glad to have found a berth and rather forgot about things as the Depression caught us all out and I joined the ranks of the unemployed. Thank God for the Royal Naval Reserve; if I hadn't joined-up I would probably have starved…

I'm sorry, you will not want to hear any of this, it is just that my life and the lives of countless other merchant seafarers were overtaken by a pretty desperate struggle just to survive.

Anyway, to return to our final arrival at the White Island. Alan Tomkins put the mokkers on too precipitate a landing and suggested that, as it was actually near midnight, we should all get some rest and make proper preparations for a landing the following day. I think he mentioned a falling glass, which was the clincher for most of us, but Hanslip kept on a bit longer, wittering about a reconnaissance. We were having a sort of pow-wow in the wardroom and it was only when Dr Crichton rather forcefully endorsed Alan's advice that Hanslip became compliant.

'We don't want anyone eaten by a polar bear do we?' I remember him remarking laconically by way of conclusion. We had seen one or two of these animals either swimming in the leads, or hauled-out on small bergs with their prey – usually some unfortunate seal.

Apart from the watch, we all turned in. Unfortunately it blew up from the west that night. By about one in the morning we had to get steam up and ease the strain on the anchor cable as the ice blew down towards us and threatened to pin us on a lee shore. It turned into a hell of a night. By two we had to get under-weigh because we risked a wrecking as the gale grew in strength and by morning it was blowing Storm Force Ten. The only thing in our favour was it was relatively warm and the movement of the ice kept breaking it up so we crawled, literally crawled, bashing our way to windward, the whole bloody ship shuddering, the rigging shaking and were about five miles off the island by 08.00 next morning.

Of course this reverse put a different complexion on everything. We three mates and our Commander were all on the bridge and Hanslip was like a petulant kid, blaming Alan for the lost opportunity. The mate quietly pointed out that had we landed a party the night before we would have been in a worse pickle as we might not have been able to recover the men. I remember I happened to be looking at Hanslip when Alan made this perfectly sensible remark and saw that it was as though Alan had struck him. It was odd, and it was some time later that I understood that the thought of actually being separated from the ship and possibly marooned, suddenly terrified our brave skipper. He blenched and I saw him swallow hard. Looking back on it, he must have been going through the agonies of hell after such a night.

As for the rest of us, we simply agreed that Alan's advice had been timely and saved us a lot of aggravation. The problem was that the storm blew for three days and we were hove-to in the ice. We were in no particular danger, for the *Alert* was a stout little ship and only occasionally did the ice really threaten us when a berg, larger than most, bore down on us from dead to windward. We actually poled off this, but we all felt its underwater body scrape down our starboard bilge. Fortunately it was rotten ice, old ice, and soft enough not to cause too much damage. Most of the time we just bumped our way through the melting pack with the occasional crash. To be truthful, having been in the Barents Sea in this present shindig, we were pretty lucky and owed a great deal more to the little barque than we knew at the time. As the gale blew the ice east and we struggled slowly west, we eventually broke clear of the pack, whereupon the seas, no longer dampened by the ice, revealed themselves as dangerous. Within hours the wind shifted to the north-west and we found ourselves pretty much on the reciprocal course to that by which we had approached the White Island, losing the very ground we had made a day or so earlier. It was all very frustrating; had any of us a proper inkling of Arctic conditions we would have taken all this in good part, but we didn't and having a ward-room full of non-seamen – the scientists and, worst of all, your father's two chaps – only exacerbated the problem. In general seamen accept the delays and vexations imposed upon them by a malign fate. They combat it by black humour and a good deal of foul-mouthed expression – catarolysis it's called and I have to say it comes in handy, keeping one's imagination at bay and hence mastering a tendency to insanity. Landsmen are quite unused to such things; everything to them is supposed to be predictable: if the 12.10 from Paddington doesn't leave until a quarter-past there are letters to *The Courier*, if you get my point. Even in wartime a degree of 'normality' is expected to prevail…

We thought that Maddox, the meteorologist and oceanographer, might have given us some advice but beyond saying that most of his polar experience had been at the other end of the globe, he managed to conclude that what we were experiencing seemed a bit odd for the time of year when high pressure was supposed to prevail in the Arctic, he proved pretty useless. To be fair he suffered another bout of sea-sickness which does nothing for a man's intellectual powers, but it further revealed the sham of our supposedly 'well-organised expedition'.

As for Commander Hanslip, he decided that the best thing for him to do was to disappear into his cabin until the gale blew itself out, leaving the ship to Alan, Nat and myself. We were pretty certain he had no source of alcohol and was just funking it all, and nothing subsequently contradicted this. Many of us had become used to our captains withdrawing into their cabins, booze or not, after the last war. A lot of them had had a pretty lousy time and the lack of national appreciation for the contribution to victory made by merchant shipping was never acknowledged. This neglect ate into them and they, and many of us younger men too, took – and continue to take - this badly. It'll be the same after this business too but, to stick to my tale, Hanslip was bloody lucky in that he had the perfectly splendid Alan Tomkins as his Chief Mate; the man seemed constantly on the move, ever thoughtful, overseeing the gear… He often went aloft himself, taking the Bosun with him, to check-out some gear that was giving us cause for concern…

He was a simply exemplary seaman, the Bosun, I mean… And I do wish I could recall his name…

Anyway, I think it was the afternoon of the day after we broke clear of the pack-ice that the fore-topsail blew out. I had the watch and had gone into the chart-room to work out a Marcq St Hilaire sight of the sun, of which I had caught a brief glimpse through the scud. It would only give me a position-line, but that was better than nothing, though the whole process was complicated by our high latitude. I was consulting the almanac when the sail went with a crack like thunder. You could feel the entire ship shaking as the damned thing, having torn free of the bolt-ropes, flogged itself to ribbons.

I had hardly reached the bridge-wing when Alan's whistle for all hands pierced the howl of the wind. Chief Mate or not – and he could have taken over from me and sent me aloft instead – Alan was first into the fore-shrouds and I have to say I watched as something of a spectator, easing the helm a bit to help the seamen that followed him onto that bucking yard. Somehow they got the remains of the wrecked sail secured and I can assure you it was no picnic. 'O'- grade canvas is dreadfully hard on the hands, more like wood than cloth, and it was unusual for it to part company with the bolt-ropes if properly made and looked after, but at least it marked the height of the storm because within an hour the wind began to drop and the glass to rise. It was such an abrupt change that at first I thought it ominous, but no, thereafter it fell away and by midnight, with a new foretopsail bent on we had reversed course and were heading back towards Kvitøya. Things move that fast in the Arctic.

The sense of relief was palpable and when I later took over from Nat under the light of the midnight sun Hanslip himself was on the bridge, writing his night orders as though the previous couple of days hadn't happened, and with a cordial 'Good night, Two-Oh,' marking the end of the episode.

The next thing I recall with any clarity is that after passing again through the pack we found the approach to Kvitøya now blocked by great humps and ridges of ice piled-up by the storm. Maddox was of the opinion that the prevailing currents would shift this in a day-or-two of fine weather and on this occasion he proved partly right, but only partly. A number of the larger, 'bergy bits' had run aground and we could not work our way inshore as closely as we had formerly, but somewhere around the last week in May we found an anchorage and veered down onto the pack so that we could get onto the ice by way of the pilot-ladder. Thereafter we began our preparations to prove whether or not that great clairvoyant, Madame Blavatskoya, was correct in her predictions.

Looking back it seems all rather unreal and bewildering. Rather ridiculous really. I suppose that if, as many wished after the blood-bath of the other sodding war, some means of reaching out beyond the physical world we are all familiar with had proved possible, we would all have thought our expedition highly successful. Now it seems verging on the stupid, even though what happened in the next few days might have persuaded a lot of people otherwise.

Nevertheless, picture us – for it had all sorts of over-laying connotations. There we were, operating in a curious world, isolated in the frozen north, on the one hand as a pseudo-scientific expedition, on the other testing the clairvoyance of an ageing white Russian *emigrée* in Hampstead. Looking back, the dilettante aspect of it all assumes even more ludicrous proportions when you set them alongside what's going on in the Western Ocean now – tonight – this very moment. A rich man's nutty project, if you'll forgive me saying so. At the time we were still thinking ourselves as cast in the Shackleton mould, brave Britons who were going to rend a *pro bono* service to the Swedes for the Good of Mankind.

Sorry if I sound unduly cynical…

I think it was the last day of May when we did get ashore, or at least the landing party did. They had a bit of struggle over the intervening ice but made it onto the White Island. The party consisted of Hanslip, of course, your father's men, Hardacre and Sykes, our three scientists, Maddox, Cronshaw and Doughty, two seamen and one of the ship's boys, the deckie, who was to act as servant, gopher and general dog's body.

There was a rather over-done handover ceremony as Hanslip, at his most pompous, conferred the great honour of command of the ship upon Alan Tomkins's more-than-broad shoulders. They then all descended onto the ice with a back-up party, organised by Nat and the Bosun, with a mountain of equipment dragged on some extemporised sledges. They looked as if bent upon reaching the pole instead of travelling little more than a mile, if that. Doc Crichton watched them go and from the bridge-wing I heard Alan remark that he was surprised that Crichton was not of the party, to which Crichton replied that 'it would not be good for the patient to be constantly under supervision' and that from what he had gleaned thus far, 'the island was not so large or inaccessible that he could not reach the landing party if sent for.' It did not seem to occur to Crichton that his help might be required at a moment's notice, nor that we might well have to beat out to sea if the weather turned against us and, oddly Alan did not emphasise this. Later he told me that he thought Crichton considered himself a bit too old to go gallivanting about on the ice and preferred his pipe, slippers and book in the cosiness of his cabin. Can't say I blamed him.

After he had got them all ashore and set up – an operation that took I think about five hours and necessitated a good deal of toing-and-froing. I think a bit of a *polynya*, a lead, opened up and I seem to recall we used the ship's rather large number of boats. I helped in the latter stages of this, then Nat returned to the ship and we three Mates, our Engineers and Marconi man sat down to a belated meal in a depleted but much relaxed wardroom.

Nat described to Alan what they had accomplished – I had seen most of it at the end of the day – as 'another British colony,' because among the tents and scientific instruments Hanslip had set up a flag-pole upon which, day-and-night up there, he could fly the good old Union Flag…

Oh, blast! There go the sirens again; we're going to have to leave it there for the night. The tale has a good way to go but we've only got one more evening and if I don't finish it by tomorrow night I'll write the rest and send it to you in the post. I happen to know that will be perfectly possible.

THE FOURTH EVENING - THE SECRET

Where were we last night? I've had a busy day… Oh, I remember, we'd just got the landing party ashore and the ship's crew proper were all back on board and looking forward to a bit of a break, if the weather allowed it. We Mates continued to keep bridge watches with a Quartermaster and a reduced deck-watch on stand-by. All rather cosy really, though our fear of another gale springing up was real enough. In fact the promised stability of high-pressure seemed to have settled in and the eventual disturbance of our brief tranquillity was entirely and horribly human.

The first inkling of trouble was the odd fact that the Union flag seemed to be upside down the following morning. It was difficult to tell, as there was little wind but Nat, ever fastidious about such points of flag etiquette – and remember that a deliberately upside-down ensign is a distress signal - pointed it out to Alan as he came up from his breakfast to relieve him. I was still having breakfast and did not have to hurry since Alan had told me at 04.00 that he would see to the ritual of winding the chronometers since our Henry was ashore. I might have had a long lie-in, but one becomes habituated to waking-up at a certain time and wake-up I had. Anyway, Alan came below for his breakfast and mentioned the oddity of the inverted Union flag.

He had just begun to say, somewhat unenthusiastically, that: 'A direct channel has opened up almost to the beach, so I suppose we had better send a boat in to see what's up,' when Nat ducked down into the ward-room.

'It's upside down all right,' he boomed, 'a breeze has got up and I'm sure of it. It was correctly hoisted last night so someone's deliberately changed it…'

'Oh fuck,' Alan said, wiping his moth and beginning to rise from the table. He had just started into his grilled bacon and I looked at Nat.

'Nat can take a boat in and have a look-see. I'll send it away Alan, you finish your breakfast. Then I'll take over the bridge.'

'Thanks. I'll be up shortly,' responded the Mate, sitting down again and motioning the ward-room steward to top-up his coffee and hasten the arrival of his toast.

Having supervised the lowering of the gig I went up to the bridge and picked up my binoculars, training them first on the distant 'flag-pole' – actually an oar, or boat-spar. There wasn't much of a breeze, which explained why it had taken some time for Nat to realise the flag had indeed been hoisted upside down. Every now and then, however, it lifted sufficiently for the fact to become clear but those ashore must have realised the probability of our not seeing it for now a cloud of dense smoke rose almost beside it. I learned afterwards that of the two able-seamen landed with Hanslip one had a Second Mate's ticket but, unable to get an officer's berth had shipped-out in the *Alert* as an AB, by no means uncommon in those days of dodgy employment opportunities. He knew that another distress signal was smoke or flames and he was clearly going for it, belt-and-braces. His name was Harris.

I felt my heart begin to race and turned my attention to the gig as it approached the shore, disappearing behind ice-hummocks before it reappeared again. Owing to the heaps of pack I had no direct line-of-sight to the beach itself but it was not long before I saw the gig coming back and it was not Nat at the tiller but, as it turned out, Able Seaman Harris who swung the gig in smartly alongside – he had been trained aboard the *Mars* I learned later – and shouted up to me to call out the Doctor.

The shouting brought Alan Tomkins on deck and smoked poor old Crichton out of his berth. 'You'd better go with him

Ned,' the Mate said as Harris further demanded our attention.

'And tell him to bring a stretcher or something!'

'Like what?'

'A fucking straight-jacket!' Harris bawled back.

'What's happened?' Alan called down to the seaman's upturned face.

'The Old Man,' Harris replied, 'he's lost his head…gone stark, staring mad!'

'Oh shit,' Alan said with quiet venom as I slid down the bridge ladder, ducked into my cabin and donned warm gear. When I got back Alan restrained me for a moment and said, 'For Christ's sake Ned, although Hanslip may be dangerous, don't forget the greater danger of polar bears.'

'Polar bears?' I recall querying rather sceptically.

'Yes,' Alan responded vehemently, 'polar bears. Now take this, just in case.' He pressed a heavy revolver into my hands. 'Stow it in your pocket but mind it, it's loaded, a chamber of six shots.' I looked at him with what have seemed like a stupid doltishness. 'And use it if you have to,' were his last words as he almost pushed me towards the rail and down the boarding ladder into the boat.

A few minutes later Crichton had scrambled down into the boat with his bag and a stretcher and a coil of heaving line had been dropped into the boat by our ever-ready Bosun – I do wish I could recall…but never mind. Harris made to relinquish the tiller to me but I motioned him to stay in charge of the boat. 'Carry on,' I said shortly, turning to the Doctor.

'Any sign of this coming on?' I asked.

Crichton shrugged. I sensed the vague shadow of the Hippocratic Oath passing over his features but Harris's announcement would be all over the ship by now. 'Not really but a relapse is possible at any time…' he said eventually.

There was no more to be said until we reached the shore and

we sat wrapped in our own thoughts as much as our duffels and woollens as the seamen strained at their oars, the sweat of effort streaming down their faces despite the cold.

'When we reach the beach get them to rub their faces clear of sweat,' I remember Crichton telling Harris.

A few moments later we swung round the shoulder of an intervening bergy-bit and the island of Kvitøya came into clear view. Low and dun-coloured, a mixture of rock, talus, broken stones, ice and the curious spectacle of pine tree boles torn out of the Siberian forests and rolled through ice and sea-water as though milled into telegraph poles which, I discovered, were a familiar sight on every open Arctic beach. But it was the sight of the landing party gathered in a little huddle that claimed our attention. Although they stood at the water's edge they seemed more intent on staring inland than watching us coming in to their assistance and it seemed each of the small knot of men held something by way of a weapon, though not one was a Lee Enfield.

It was Nat who grabbed the gig's stem-head and eased her impetus as her velocity drove her against the shingle. I was out of her and alongside him in a second as the crew helped the less agile Crichton ashore.

'Well?' I asked curtly.

Nat's face was pale and drawn. 'Hanslip's lost his bloody marbles and has run amok. He's running around with a boat-axe. He's already…' Nat made a gesture, directing my gaze to the ground.

'Christ!' I said looking down to where the deck-boy lay almost among the very feet on the entire landing party. The lad was covered in blood and, from a quick glance it seemed as if his right arm was almost severed at the shoulder.

'Hanslip?'

'Well, it wasn't a fucking polar bear.'

It was clear now why the men had gathered in a group, partly to protect themselves and each other, but also to protect the deck-boy. 'The bastard cut him down for no apparent reason. They've staunched the worst of the bleeding…'

By now Crichton was out of the boat and aware of the situation; the men made way for him. He knelt beside the boy, opened his bag and began work.

'Where are the guns?' I asked, referring to the Lee Enfields landed to protect the landing party from polar bears.

'I dunno,' Nat responded. 'haven't had time to…'

'They were in one of the tents, sir,' offered Harris, who was now ashore alongside us. 'We tried getting to them but Commander Hanslip was too clever for us…'

I was thinking fast. There was no actual sign of Hanslip, but I could hear a strange sound, a sort of anguished roaring which every now and again rose to a scream before subsiding for a while.

'Where is he?'

Nat shrugged but Maddox the meteorologist drew me to one side, out of the hearing of the men, most of whom were fixated on Crichton's efforts to keep the little deck-boy alive. The poor little chap's face was deathly pale.

Once we were clear of the group gathered round Crichton and his patient, Maddox confided a breathless torrent of information: 'The witch Blavatskoya is right! The Swedes are here alright and it's not a pretty sight. We stumbled on them this morning whilst going out to take some observations, then let the Commander know. We didn't disturb them or anything, thinking that he ought to be told first. He came hurrying up, waved us aside telling us to get on with our work and went into their tent…'

'It's still intact?'

'Well, not really, but they're under what's left of it…'

'And then?'

'I don't know, we sort of hung back, out of curiosity, I suppose, and a good deal of apprehension, then Hanslip emerged white as a sheet. Geoffrey here, and John…' Maddox indicated Hardacre and Sykes, the *Courier's* team, 'had come up and…'

'We went up to Hanslip who flew at us. He had a rifle in his hand and fired it at me, telling me keep away and fuck off. I backed-off quickly, as did the others…'

'Shaken by this we turned back to our camp on the beach…' Maddox hesitated, then went on, 'we had forgotten we had taken the deck-boy with us…he's a bright lad and…' Maddox paused again mastering powerful emotion. 'It all happened so fast, Adams, you have to understand,' he said insistently.

'Tell me what happened so fast,' I pressed him, by heart thudding in my chest.

Maddox gulped then went on: 'Derek Cronshaw suddenly asked "where's the deckie?" and…' the poor man was choking on his words, 'there was a shout and then a scream. Hardacre turned back and then we saw the lad stumbling after us, covered in blood… He was just able to say "The Captain, the Captain…" before he collapsed at our feet as a shot whistled over our heads. We got him down here on the beach, hoisted the ensign upside down and then Harris here said we should get some oil alight…'

I was thinking fast and I asked Maddox, 'so only you three Boffins, the two *Courier* boys and the deckie saw the Swedes?'

'Eh?'

'You heard me Maddox…'

'Er,' Maddox frowned. He was in deep shock. 'Yes, yes, that's right…' he said after pulling himself together.

'Now where is the place where you found the Swedes?' I recall asking and Maddox pointed. 'Right,' I said, 'now you go and get your two colleagues and tell them from me if they mention one word of what they saw to another member of the crew I'll have their guts for garters – and I mean that.' Maddox nodded, a man almost palpably relieved – at least partially - of a burden.

We walked rapidly back to rest of them. I exchanged glances with Nat Gardner and then turned to Crichton.

'Can you save the boy?' I asked.

Crichton looked up, 'I don't know. He's already lost a lot of blood…'

'Let's get you and the boy back to the ship,' I said turning to the men round us. 'Get him on the stretcher and into the gig as quickly as possible. We'll try and contain Hanslip…'

Crichton rose to his feet grabbed my elbow and tugged me out of the group. 'You don't understand Adams,' he said with an air of ferocity. 'It's Hanslip we have to worry about. His actions could be highly unpredictable. One possibly mortally wounded boy is nothing to what havoc he might wreak if we leave him to his own devices with a gun…'

They were lifting the deck-boy into the boat.

'You're going to have to leave Hanslip to me, Doc,' I said with what patience I could muster. I turned to Able Seaman Harris.

'But,' he protested, only to be cut short by Nat.

'If Hanslip shot that boy, Doc, you'd be helping the Old Man by saving the lad.' The implication of murder hung heavily in the charged air.

Crichton grunted and turned back to the boat, muttering something about leaving matters in the wrong hands.

'Harris,' I said firmly, thankful for Nat's intelligent intervention, 'get the doctor and his patient back to the ship. The rest of you follow. When we get back with the Old Man we'll decide what's to be done next. Now, Nat, Hardacre and Sykes come with me.'

Derek Cronshaw raised an objection but I looked meaningfully at Maddox, saying, 'just do what I fucking say!' and, as Maddox motioned to Cronshaw and Jim Doughty aside, I drew off Nat and the two men from *The Courier*.

'Now listen, you two,' I said addressing Hardacre and Sykes, 'I know you are news-paper men but just for once forget it. Under the Merchant Shipping Act you are under my orders as super-numeraries and you will not take any action with regard to what you may be about to see until the matter has been resolved aboard the *Alert*. D'you understand? And, for what it is worth, I want your word on it…'

'But Adams it's our job…' Sykes was waving his camera.

'Fuck your job and fuck your camera. There could be serious repercussions about all this…' I looked at the two of them. Unsurprisingly resentment burned in their eyes, they were on the edge of the scoop of a lifetime – with no responsibility as to the outcome. I looked at Nat. 'This goes for you too, Mr Gardner,' I said formally.

Nat grasped the significance of my meaning sufficiently to respond with a crisp, 'Absolutely, sir.'

I turned back to the other two. 'Your word…'

'Until we get back to the ship, but no longer,' said Hardacre, and Sykes grunted agreement.

'Right, that's settled then. Now, show me where the Swedes are.'

Neither of the newspapermen moved. 'Look Adams, the skipper's out there off his trolley with at least four loaded Lee Enfields. If I can't do my job, I'm certainly not going to do yours for you.'

For a moment I was nonplussed. I can't think why, Hardacre's argument was entirely plausible, but I was growing angry and losing the capacity to reason clearly. Thank God Nat again stepped into the breach.

'Well, you two had better get back to the ship then. Go on; just point us in the right direction.'

Hardacre indicated the place. We all turned; there was no sign of anything except the low rise of the land but then I thought I detected a movement on the skyline.

'There he is!' Sykes exclaimed.

'Good,' said Nat, 'and I'll take that camera!'

Before Sykes could even react Nat Gardner had wrenched the big Hasselblad off Sykes and was off over the broken ground.

'Hey! You bastard!' I put up a hand to stop Sykes running after Nat.

'You're going back to the ship,' I snapped, 'now!'

'If he damages that camera…'

I left the two of them fuming and made after Nat. He was unarmed and vulnerable. I caught up with him and said 'thanks.'

'Pair of idiots,' Nat said shortly, looking back. The two newspapermen were walking back to the beach, though Sykes looked over his shoulder at us. 'What are we going to do about..?'

And at that point there was a gun-shot, then another. I don't know where the bloody shots went but I do know that within a few moments every man-jack on that stony beach was either in a boat or pushing and shoving to get them afloat.

Nat turned to me and said, 'as I was saying…'

I confess I was totally nonplussed. It was clear that Hanslip was shooting to kill and we needed time to think and to consult, the revolver in my duffel-coat notwithstanding. I was no shot, least of all with a hand-gun. 'Come on,' I said, waving to Nat to follow.

We ran back down towards the beach, shouting for the others to wait but we were too late, the boats were all pulling hard for the ship, not easing until the large bergy-bits were between them and the island. By which time a bullet had ricocheted off a rock close to us and both of us lay flat on our faces.

I remember Nat swearing and my own heart hammering. A silence followed then Nat said, 'well the Hasselblad's good and properly fucked.' A big chap, he'd fallen heavily on top of the camera and smashed the lens and done goodness knows what other damage.

For a long moment we lay there staring stupidly at one another then Nat said, 'did someone say Hanslip's got *four* rifles?'

'Yes, I think so… and I've got this…' I pulled out the revolver Alan Tomkins had pressed on me.

'That's something, I suppose, but to my mind if we are not outnumbered, we're still out-gunned.'

I don't know for how many minutes we lay there, caught in the web of fear and indecision, but a further gunshot found us pressed to the ground until Nat observed, 'I don't think that went anywhere near us…'

There was a sudden scream, the noise of a man in terror and I knew intuitively that Hanslip was in trouble himself. I got up and at a low lope ran up the low slope with Nat close behind me.

The White Island stretched ahead of us, stark and bare of any vegetation except coloured lichens on the rocks and boulders and on the far side of a fast-flowing rivulet of melt-water the remains of an extemporised tent stood. I do not know of what it was constructed, presumably the balloon fabric, or how those three desperate men had contrived to carry it from the wreckage of their balloon gondola. It was an equal mystery as to how this extemporised shelter had withstood decades of Arctic gales, I really have no very clear memory of any of these details largely because what we found inside, or underneath, for I think the whole thing had collapsed, etched itself on the mind to the exclusion of other details…

You know four years ago I would have needed a stiff drink

before telling you the rest of this but, after the horrors of the North Atlantic, what we saw that afternoon seems now to be but overture and beginners…

Anyhow the three Swedish adventurers, or what remained of them, lay there in conditions one can only describe as squalid. There were some syringes lying about and one of them was wrapped in what remained of the Swedish flag. It was clear they had shot themselves full of something - opium we supposed later, for there was precious little evidence of food, tinned or otherwise, though a bear's skeleton lay about twelve feet away, so it was clear that they had sustained themselves for a while on that. There were two smooth-bore Remingtons lying nearby to show how. But that wasn't the worst of it. Other bears had been at them, of course; in fact a great deal of them had been clearly eaten by polar bears, Arctic foxes or Burgomeister gulls, but one corpse - we had no way of knowing one from another - had his thigh muscles carved smooth and the offending knife lay beside one of the cadavers' right hands – or what remained thereof. It looked as though one of them had expired and the other two had decided to eat him; perhaps they had drawn lots and dispatched the wretch – it was all conjecture, but Nat put the name to it and it almost coloured the very air we breathed and we found it choking.

'Cannibalism,' he said in a low voice. There were the remains of a small cooking fire just outside the collapsed tent. The whole thing was utterly pathetic and preserved in that odd way the polar regions retain the past for years after the event..

The poor devils had partly decomposed, thawing out a bit each summer, but the smell was not unduly offensive and in fact their state of preservation – given their mauling by bears and so forth - was remarkable. Nevertheless, I found myself gagging and Nat was retching. Both of us had to turn away, whereupon we heard the noise, a low keening, a strangely sad, plaintive sound, rather, I thought, like that made by seals when they haul themselves out of the sea on a rock and beguiling enough to convince the mariners of old that they were hearing the song of the sirens.

Nat was less of a romantic, 'What the fuck…?' he said, but we knew the source of the dirge, for that is what it was. Hanslip wasn't far off. We turned our attention away from the sad wreckage of the three Swedish adventurers' expedition and Nat began to inch forward.

'Careful, Nat,' I recall saying. 'He can't be far away and I think there are bears about.'

'That's bloody obvious…' We were both in a high state of tension but then Nat saw the rifle. 'He's left one of them here.' Nat wriggled towards the Lee Enfield and drew back the bolt. 'There's one shot at least,' he said, his voice now low and his tone determined.

We both began to edge forward on our bellies, approaching a second low rise in the land. It is surprising how little one can see when pressed to the ground but Nat suddenly hissed: 'There he is!'

I spotted him at almost the same instant, off to our left. He was down on all fours his body swaying from side-to-side, apparently oblivious to our presence.

'Oh, God…' It was all too obvious why he had abandoned his interest in taking pot-shots at us. He was staring at a large polar bear which had clearly already mauled him, for we could see blood pouring from his head and face. But he had scored a hit on the bear, which was also bleeding. Alongside me Nat brought his Lee Enfield up to his shoulder. My heart was in my mouth; I hoped there were no other bears about, for if Nat only had one shot, while it might knock down the wounded animal I didn't hold out much reliance on my expertise with a revolver as helping.

The Lee Enfield cracked beside me and the bear's head went sideways with the impact. The great beast swayed for a moment then fell sideways, stone dead.

Cautiously we got to our feet. As we moved forward Hanslip stared at the dead bear, then turned and saw us approaching, both with guns in our hands. I don't know what we expected except it was not this wreckage of a man cringing at our feet. He looked up at us the tears streaming down his face, the left cheek of which was half torn away, the blood fairly pouring onto a small patch of scurvy grass; his bare hands were blue with cold, I remember, inconsequentially.

I heard Nat murmur 'Jesus Christ' and thought we must get this half-man, half wild-beast back to the ship as soon as possible, before more bears, attracted by the smell of blood, caught us out.

Hanslip tried to say something but his mutilated mouth prevented anything comprehensible from emerging. Nat thought it was something like 'you left me to die…' but I couldn't say for certain.

'We're going to get you back to the ship, sir,' I remember saying as Nat and I both took him under an armpit and got him half to his feet. Somehow, unmolested by bears, we half-dragged, half-carried him over the broken ground until the beach lay before us.

About fifty yards off the gig was approaching with Crichton in it and as we lay our burden down just short of the tideline, Crichton was beside Hanslip with his bag.

'The Mate sent us back in for you, sir,' Harris explained as we stood aside, alternately casting glances over our shoulder for bears, whilst Crichton ministered to his charge.

'What about the deck-boy?' I asked.

Harris shook his head. 'Not looking good, sir. He's lost a lot of blood despite the tourniquet.'

Crichton was having a sort of meaningless conversation with Hanslip. I heard him say something like: 'I think so, Henry, don't you…'

Then Hanslip meekly held out a wrist and Crichton shoved the clothing back as far as it would go. I watched the poor bastard's eyes close and an expression of profound relief cross his face as Crichton shot him full of morphia or opium or something similar.

'Let's have that stretcher,' Crichton snapped as he applied a field dressing to Hanslip's mauled face.

Once back at the ship we left Crichton to his patients in the sick-bay and Nat and I stopped Alan from calling a conference in the ward-room and took him into my cabin, Nat following. The door was secured and Alan asked: 'Well? What in the name of God happened?'

'Well the prediction by the clairvoyant was right…'

'I know that,' he said curtly, 'as for the rest, everyone's being very coy.'

I avoided Nat's eyes. 'That's because I told the five men who actually saw the Swedes to keep their traps shut…'

I didn't get any further; there was a violent banging on the door which Nat opened to see a furious and white-faced Sykes demanding to know what had happened to his precious Hasselblad.

'I fell on it,' Nat said simply. 'It's smashed to smithereens, the lens has gone…'

'You bastard! You did it deliberately…'

'No, I didn't. But I was going to. As it happened it was an accident. I'm sure you have it insured. Now, if you don't mind…' Nat shut the door in Sykes's face and we stood in silence as we listened to Sykes railing in the ward-room about the arrogance of ship's officers.

'Go on,' Alan Tomkins prompted me. I told him about the

state of the Swedish encampment, the syringes and the evidence of cannibalism. 'On the grounds that none of this adduces to the honour of the Swedish nation I thought it right and proper to limit the number of people who knew anything about it. In the end, it is not up to me, but it seemed that there, on that island, with Hanslip running amok, we had our hands full. As this was largely a goodwill mission it seemed to me best to draw a veil over the whole sorry episode, especially as Hanslip had shot the deck-boy…'

'While the balance of his was disturbed,' Alan finished the sentence for me.

'Yes, certainly, but how is that going to play out if it is made public that old Southmoore sent a ship up into the Arctic under the command of a known madman.'

'Was he known?'

'There wasn't to be a quack on board until someone had second thoughts.'

'True,' Alan conceded.'

'The Second Mate's right, sir,' Nat said.

Tomkins blew out his cheeks. I shall need to talk to Crichton but if you are suggesting that we hush the whole matter up, how the hell are we going to keep the crew from talking?'

'I doubt they will be a problem,' I said. 'Once we get home and primed with our version of events they'll split to the four winds and no-one will take much notice of the odd yarn…'

'*Our version of events?*' Tomkins was rueful rather than outraged, 'and what is that going to be, eh?'

'We should mention Hanslip's alcoholism mental instability, blaming it upon stress and shell-shock from the late war. Being Hanslip he went off exploring on his own hoping to be the first to accomplish tour mission, taking the deck-boy – he probably wanted his doggie, you know how he was about these things – and they ran into bears attracted to the beach by our scent. A bear got to the boy then Hanslip was attacked. He completely lost his nerve, got himself mauled, he's got the marks to prove it if he survives…' I paused a moment and then added somewhat brutally, 'and now you're really in command and you'll be writing the report of proceedings.' I was a bit brutal.

'Hm,' Tomkins said after digesting my suggestion. 'How the hell did you think all that through?'

I shrugged. 'How else are we going to present it?'

'And what about the Blavatskoya thing?'

I shrugged again. 'Let's just go home,' I remember saying. I expect it was delayed shock after the tension of our adventure but I do recall feeling that I really did not care about Madame Blavatskoya and that the whole enterprise was an exercise in condescension and futility. The fact that a clairvoyant had worked out that we would find the three Swedish bodies on Kvitøya was probably not so very far-fetched. As was well-known, Nansen had discovered polar drift and the clairvoyant's prediction did not mean that every – or any – family bereaved by the horrors of the last war were going to be able to speak to their lost kith and kin.

'Would you like me to muster all hands and get the encampment broken-up?' Nat had asked. Alan appeared to consider the matter then looked at my cabin clock. It registered five to three. 'That's afternoon,' he said, 'though it seems like far later. Yes, muster the hands and get all the boats we can man to withdraw all the gear as quickly as possible. We'll gather in the wardroom when the work's done…'

'Job and finish, sir?' asked Nat, using the phrase that meant no break until the task was accomplished.

'Job and finish,' Alan confirmed. 'And try and bring the guns back,' he added hopefully.

There followed several hours of relentless activity. Nat, armed with his Lee Enfield and backed-up by Harris with what had been Hanslip's rifle, went in search of the other guns and picked them all up without revisiting the Swedish encampment and drawing Harris's attention to it, partially hidden as it was. Twice, Nat told me later, polar bears had appeared, attracted by our smell, no doubt, but a judicial gunshot or two had scared them off.

The rest of us toiled on the beach to dismantle the camp and, with the last of the boats full of gear, we were soon pulling away from the stony beach for the last time. I looked back once, just before the large bergy-bit closed the view of the tideline and saw it as I see it now in my mind's eye, a remote, almost inaccessible stretch of Arctic wilderness, best left to the bears and the foxes, the ptarmigans and the hares and whatever creatures are better suited to inhabit it than man.

As we came alongside we were met with the news that the deck-boy had died. It was the Bosun who broke it as we clambered over the rail; there were tears in his eyes, I remember. 'He was my sister's boy,' he said simply. I had had no idea…

Anyway, there was a huge tureen of ham and pea soup on the wardroom table. The smell of it brought some warmth back into our bodies and Alan insisted we all had a tot in memory of the lad. 'To little Jamie,' he said, and I realised that apart from seeing his name on the crew list as 'J.M. Dell,' I had taken scant notice of the boy, but Alan had and that was typical of the man.

More personally cheering was Alan's news that he had spoken to Crichton and the Doc had agreed with me. Nothing was to be gained by revealing what we had found of the Swedes, he had told Alan, and he had reached very much the same conclusion as had I when it came to establishing the legitimacy of Blavatskoya's claim. He was, after all, a man of science. I said as much to Alan who smiled wryly.

'Sir Arthur Conan Doyle was a man of science, Ned,' he said, 'and he served as a quack in an Arctic whaler, but it didn't stop him believing in fairies.'

'*Touché*,' I remember responding, adding, 'but the Doc doesn't come out of this as squeaky clean, you know.'

Alan considered this for a moment and then shook his head. 'You're an ingenious bastard,' he said to me with half a smile.

That evening, with Hanslip secured in his cabin and a seaman posted outside with orders to call one of the Mates and the Doctor if he heard anything, the rest of the senior ship's staff – including all the super-numeraries, *The Courier*'s boys and the boffins – assembled in the wardroom.

Alan Tomkins punctiliously read out the entry he had made in the *Alert*'s Official Log-Book. He had more-or-less followed my advice, setting down a version of events that seemed to him kinder to all concerned. Not mentioning the complete mental break-down of the Master, but that on landing he had unwisely wandered off in search of any sign of the Swedish expedition with the Deck Boy as his runner, only to encounter polar bears, one of which attacked and mortally wounded young Dell whilst he himself suffered a grievous mauling. Tomkins went on to say that Commander Hanslip's condition rendered him unfit for service and that under such circumstances, he, Alan Tomkins, was taking command of the auxiliary barque *Alert*. He carefully copied the number of his Certificate of Competence and signed the Certificate of Registry to the same effect. Able Seaman John Harris, being in possession of a Certificate of Competence as Second Mate was promoted to Acting Third Mate.

The he quietly asked: 'Do any of you dissent from this account?'

I looked at Hardacre and Sykes. They were clearly unhappy with the situation they found themselves in and Hardacre said shortly, 'yes; it's a pack of lies.'

Alan's face flushed. He could expect obedience from Nat and

myself, even a degree of compliance from the scientists, but with the newshounds it was a very different matter. It was Nat who came to Alan's rescue.

'That's droll coming from a journalist,' he said drily.

'I'm not going to let sleeping dogs lie,' Hardacre persisted and Sykes added: 'As for you, you bastard, you sabotaged my camera.'

'I told you it was an accident,' Nat maintained coolly.

'What d'you think, Doc?' Hardacre asked Crichton, appealing to the chief non-nautical man on board. The Doctor had been even more withdrawn since leaving the beach and seemed to suddenly shrink as all eyes turned on him for a final judgement.

'I agree with our new Captain,' Crichton said simply, adding with a deep flushing, 'and I have the ear and the confidence of Lord Southmoore…' Not even I had thought of that clincher, but I could tell that neither Hardacre nor Sykes were going to take all this lying down. However, for the moment Crichton held the advantage and asked Tomkins, 'It's proper to put a diagnosis in the Official Log is it not?'

'Er, yes,' Alan responded, the tone of his voice cautious.

'Well, it may be asked why Commander Hanslip went off on his own. I think you used the verb "wandered," did you not, sir?'

'I did,' Alan replied.

'Well then if you sign the log entry, I will witness it and that Commander Hanslip had been suffering from tarassis…'

'What the hell is that?' asked Hardacre incredulously.

'Male hysteria, Mr Hardacre. A new word for your journalistic vocabulary, no doubt.'

Tomkins and Crichton both bent over the Official Log Book and I witnessed both signatures. The deed was done.

'Thank you Patrick,' Tomkins said looking up at the Chief Engineer. 'Mr Jones, will you be good enough to raise steam. We'll need your engines to clear the land. I think that it is time we all went home.'

I wish I could say that the story ended there but, of course, it didn't. Neither Hardacre nor Sykes were to be so easily placated and, as it turned out, Dr Patrick Crichton had his own agenda. We cleared the ice, our ensign at half-mast until we had buried Jimmie Dell. Thereafter the mood of the ship's company lifted a little, as it always does when homeward bound, even if that did mean probable unemployment; first there would be a pay-off and money in hand – that was the way of things.

Anyway, we were two days into our homeward passage, bowling along under easy sail somewhere off Edgeøya, the boilers banked at two hours' notice when, at dinner that night, the Doc came into the wardroom and announced that Hanslip had taken a turn for the worse.

'He has developed a high fever and I am not optimistic,' he said shortly, 'Despite my best efforts, his wound is infected. He sat down and pulled his serviette from its ring.

Being now the *Alert*'s Chief Mate I was on my way up to the bridge at four the following morning and paused outside Hanslip's cabin. After Dell's death we had moved him back into the Master's accommodation and I could hear him muttering deliriously. We had removed the seaman from guard-duty so I opened the door and stuck my head inside, just to see if all was well, or as well as it could be. Crichton was beside him and he was administering something by intravenous injection. The Doc realised I had popped my head into the cabin and turned towards me. He seemed startled to see me but that was not altogether surprising. Anyway, he shook his head as if to say Hanslip was a bad way and I assumed he was giving Hanslip an analgesic but from the sequel I am now all but certain that it was a lethal dose for at 06.00 Tomkins, now our Commander, of course, came up on the bridge and told me that Crichton had told him that Hanslip was dead.

I didn't make any connection between the two events except that Crichton failed to join us at breakfast that morning. Nor was he at lunch or dinner. I asked Alan if he was all right.

'He's upset,' Alan explained, 'very upset. He's lost two patients, one of them being the man whom he was supposed to nurture through thick and thin. At his request I've had him served his meals in his cabin.'

I didn't think to connect Crichton's conduct that morning with anything sinister, simply because at that time I was not suspicious but a few nights later – I say nights because we had crossed the Arctic Circle and there were a few hours when it grew darker than we had become accustomed to – Crichton began to mess with us again and the following night, at dinner, Hardacre and Sykes kicked-off in the ward-room. They must have been stewing for days but they made it quite clear that they intended to repudiate any sort of obligation Tomkins or I had laid them under, and told Crichton to his face.

Now you have to understand that, like David Manners, our Sparkie, I was on watch at the time, while Tomkins had not yet gone into the ward-room for dinner, so I only had this second hand but it was played out in front of Nat Gardner, Owen Jones, Second Engineer Rayne, and the three Boffins: Maddox, Cronshaw and Doughty. Perhaps the absence of Tomkins emboldened the two newspaper men. Anyway, without uttering a word, Crichton apparently rose from the table and withdrew into his cabin, shutting the sliding door with a click so that Nat thought he had locked himself in.

'That's told him,' Hardacre said with what Nat thought of as 'gloating satisfaction,' looking round the table and announcing that: 'you bastards are not going to get away with this just to protect a drunken skipper…'

'You should watch your tongue,' Nat apparently warned Hardacre.

'And you can shut your fucking mouth,' Hardacre snapped, at which point Crichton's cabin door flew back, he levelled a revolver at Hardacre and shot him in the head. According to Nat, as Hardacre crashed backwards all hell broke loose. Crichton fired next at Sykes and then, to quote Nat, 'he again withdrew into his cabin, slammed the door and blew out his own brains.'

The noise of the gun-shots, screams of the victims and shouts of the others, conjoined with the clatter of crockery and cutlery falling to the deck, brought Tomkins out of his cabin, where, it transpired, he had fallen asleep and left the quartermaster and myself on the bridge in a lather of curiosity and insecurity… In the end I went below to where Nat was trying his best to save Sykes, I think it was.

That's it, really. We brought the little barque home and the crew were all paid off, most of them cursing the voyage, the ship and, most likely, the whole sorry enterprise. I have no idea what happened to the scientific staff beyond that vague memory of some sort of scientific paper, but *The Courier* carried a short piece about the expedition being aborted owing to the mental distress of the Doctor who had taken the lives 'of several of the ship's company'. It made no waves because your father had a bigger news story to cover; the depression that had infected shipping had just got worse; there was a serious strike by British merchant seamen already in progress Down Under and then the General Strike was upon us to claim all the headlines. As for the clairvoyant rubbish, well, as you well know, general interest in such things evaporated and shortly after matters went from bad to worse with the Wall Street Crash, some sealers discovered the secret of Kvitøya, the White Island, in 1930, I think.

*

'You know the rest,' he said, sitting back in his chair and lighting another cigarette. All-in-all, it was a bit of a bloody shambles.'

He smiled wanly at her as she closed her notebook and looked up at him. He was hoarse with talking, but it seemed to her that he had the face of a man younger than he had been upon their first encounter. Was it only five nights ago? It seemed far longer.

'Well, thank you for your candour,' she said. 'You have been very helpful and my father will be most grateful to you.'

He shrugged and, for the first time, smiled at her properly. It revealed again that deeply concealed kindness, wiping away the cynicism and the hurt and the war-weariness.

'Truth to tell, Lizzie,' he said, using her name for the very first time and drawing on his cigarette as he leaned forward towards her in a posture of sudden intimacy, 'relating all this in your company has done me good. Taken my mind off other things and stopped me brooding. *I'm* grateful for *that*.

'You *were* something of a misanthrope,' she said, smiling.

'I'm sure I was…'

'I think that you ought to know that Hal Hanslip, as he was known, was actually my father's half-brother. Doctor Crichton was also a relative, my mother's cousin.

'Oh, I see,' he said, leaning back in his chair nodding. So Southmoore had given his alcoholic half-brother a chance and the wretched fellow had blown it. 'And do you know quite why…?

'Why what he saw in that tent brought on the final fit of insanity, and why he had taken to drink in the first place? Yes, I do.' Her face grew clouded and for the first time he saw the sensitive woman that lay beneath the tough façade of the reporter. With a sudden pang she reminded him again of Moira.

'Will you tell me?' he asked softly.

She nodded, lifting up her empty glass, which he refilled.

'You recall he was involved in the Allied Intervention in

Northern Russia in 1919? Well, he had some dealings ashore, in charge of a naval party in Archangel where he met a young Russian woman. You will not need me to tell you that we, and particularly the Scots shipping and mercantile houses, did a lot of business with North Russia before the Bolshevik Revolution. He had a letter of introduction from a cousin in the trade to a merchant in Archangel and by this contact formed a liaison with a young woman named Alexandrovna. During the terrible and turbulent months that followed, they lost touch, then Uncle Hal got ashore again towards the end of the Intervention and went in search of her. I gather he overstayed his leave and would have been cashiered had he not escaped…'

'He was captured by the Bolsheviks?'

She nodded. 'He got cut off, then found himself with a small group of White Russians, mostly dispossessed men who had lost everything except their hunting rifles. Uncle Hal was with them in a desperate last stand as the Bolsheviks smoked them out of a barn and then fought them in four days of pursuit through the forest. They were all shot, except him, his British naval uniform saving him and eventually he was exchanged, but by that time he had almost lost his mind and was more of an embarrassment to the Bolsheviks who didn't want a major incident just as the Allies were pulling out of North Russia and abandoning the Whites…'

'I'm not surprised, having been to Uncle Joe's Workers' Paradise,' he interjected. 'But there's more, isn't there?'

'Yes. What turned him into an alcoholic was, quite by chance when retreating through the forest, finding Alexandrovna…' she paused, then shuddered, adding, 'or what was left of her…'

'Just like the Swedes?'

She nodded. 'Whether it was dogs, wolves or, as he maintained, hungry humans…' She went no further for it was not necessary to do so. The grisly image hung between them as they stared at each other, then she shook her head and he emptied the bottle into their glasses.

'What a fucking world,' he murmured half to himself.

She took a long drink and then said, brightly, 'Changing the subject, I gather congratulations are in order.'

He frowned, drawing himself away from her, suddenly the angry man she had first met. 'How the hell…?'

She laid her right hand on his left arm as he ground out the cigarette in the ashtray that lay between them. 'I somewhat misled you on our first meeting. I do have a spy in Uncle Max's den,' she said coolly, 'a school-friend in the Wrens… She works at Derby House.''

'Christ on a bike!'

It was as though the revelation about Hanslip and the fact that she knew all about his personal news returned them to the exact point of their first encounter. This lasted for no more than a few seconds, as their lives drew apart again.

'Anyway, it's in the *Gazette*, so congratulations, *Commander*,' she said, laying heavy emphasis on his new rank. 'You might as well look pleased. Promotion *and* a decoration. And both well deserved.'

He shrugged. 'Well, the promotion, perhaps, but one doesn't kill U-boats on one's own, there's my whole ship's company…without them I'm just a stuffed shirt…' He forbore saying that he had now reached the elevated status of her Uncle Hal. 'What are you laughing about?' he asked.

'You must be the first naval officer to admit that. Isn't the usual line: "I got the gong on behalf of you all?" ' She finished the sentence with a put-on pompous male voice.

It was his turn to laugh as he relaxed again.

They found themselves suddenly tongue-tied and staring at each other, their hands close on the napery. Then, without moving, he seemed to retreat inside himself again, his eyes no longer focussed upon her face but, still staring at her, gazing at something far beyond her. She flushed and said quietly:

'It would be nice if we could do this again, in different circumstances.'

He frowned and looked at her again. 'I'm sorry, what did you say? I was miles away.'

'I said it would be nice if we could do this again, in different circumstances... Have dinner together...'

'Oh. Yes...yes, it would, but...' He hesitated, as if making to say more than merely shook his head.

'Go on.'

'I can't,' he said simply, 'Not that I don't want to, but I simply can't, Lizzie, not until this bloody war is over, and God alone knows when that might be, or whether we will both live to see an end to it...or what that end might be...'

They sat staring at each other for some minutes, then she sniffed and nodded, raising her near emptied glass, said thickly, 'To the end of the war then.'

He smiled, his eyes suddenly compassionate and moved by the tears in hers. 'Yes. To the end of the war.'

The chink of their glasses was drowned as the air-raid sirens began to sound their dismal alarm.

Out in the darkened street full of hurrying people he held out his hand. 'To the end of the war,' he said again and she repeated the mantra. Then they parted only for him to turn back, an instant later and call: 'Lizzie!'

She had almost disappeared in the crowd but she turned and he closed the distance between them. 'It has just come to me,' he said smiling sadly.

'What has?' she asked almost gaily, he thought afterwards, as if glad that their parting had been delayed.

'The name of the *Alert*'s Bosun,' he replied with a chuckle.

'What was it?'

‘Tucker,’ he said, ‘Thomas Tucker. How on earth could a seaman forget a name like that, eh?’

LONDON, MAY 1945.

He emerged from the station into full daylight; the dark bulk of the Euston arch rose against the sky and he stopped, blinking with exhaustion. He had slept fitfully on the train, just as he had slept fitfully for the last five and a half years, unable now to break the habit of what seemed a lifetime – yet was not.

He felt himself sway like a drunk and made the effort to steady himself. What in God's name was he doing here in London, but chasing some chimera? A crazy Quixotic notion, conceived in the heady hour of victory when the triumphant young officers attending the wardroom party to which he had, by convention, been invited, asked him 'what shall you do now, sir?'

It was a moot point. Most of them were reservists of one sort or another, eager to get back to their interrupted careers; he could only shrug, smile graciously and respond 'go back to sea, I suppose,' swapping the command of one of His Majesty's frigates for perhaps a Chief Officer's job on a cargo-liner whence he had come.

But the bone weariness would have to be overcome first, for he did not believe he could function without proper rest. He had seen enough men crack during the struggle for supremacy in the North Atlantic, the years of unrelenting toil, of having to win not once, but twice after the enemy revived the struggle with new advanced technologies in the autumn of forty-three after almost six months of what seemed the palm of victory having been awarded to the Allied cause.

So why come to London? True his childhood home had been in its outer suburbs, but that had all gone now, swept away by war, his parents dead, the old house sold. After the death of Moira and her unborn child in the wild, 'friendly-fire' bombing in West Hendon, he had reverted to being the itinerant seafarer, as he had been when in the Merchant Service, a man bound to his ship, never the shore. The shore was for playing upon, for brief, heady interludes of whatever madness one could afford; a fling; a binge; sometimes – but rarely - a real holiday. And then the war had come and as a reservist he had been called to the colours and quickly been appointed to command a corvette. The rusty little war-bucket *Nemesia* had sunk a U-boat and earned Lieutenant Commander Edward Adams a DSC and promotion to Commander. The brass hat came with a brand new frigate and command of an escort group which had bagged two more U-boats and added a bar to his decoration. There had been wardroom parties, congratulations, even a visit from the Commander-in-Chief, Western Approaches, Admiral Horton himself, but all that was over. The frigate lay in dry-dock being prepared for service in the Far East, his own future in her uncertain. All that was certain was that he had three weeks leave ahead of him before he must give her another thought.

So what could he think about? All the conscious wisdom of his age and experience told him to rest. He had fantasised about withdrawing into the country, Cheshire somewhere, or North Wales, the fastness of Snowdonia – anywhere away from the smell of hot oil, steam, rust, and the noise of the sea, or a ship-yard, or even the banal chatter of a wardroom where he felt he might at any moment slap the cheery red faces of young naval officers wallowing in excessive amounts of gin to toast the defeat of Germany. They had done him proud, though, a wonderful troop of amateurs-turned-sea-warriors. The only person requiring a slap was himself; get yourself away from all this before you add to the number of men broken by the battle for the Atlantic, for already it was clear that the great conflict of the Western Ocean would sink under the glamorous supremacy of other theatres, better comprehended by the British public. The Spitfire was the war's icon, along with the Brylcream boys who flew it, that much was clear now. What - it would soon be asked – was a corvette? And what did the Merchant Navy do in the war; and what was it anyway?

All these bitter convictions had seeped into his soul but he could not quite drown them in liquor as others did, nor fuck his wits into stupidity, not after Moira. And so, a week after VE-Day, he had donned a civvie suit and followed his own foot-steps to Lime Street station to board a train for London.

Now he stood blinking in the morning light, staring up at the great arch and asked himself 'where now?'

But, of course he knew. It was a long and very foolish shot that he was taking and the next thing to be decided was how to take it. He watched a bus move east along the Euston Road, shook his head at the soliciting cabbie at the head of the taxi rank and made to walk along the road towards King's Cross and a small hotel he had occasionally used. Here he dumped his hold-all and secured a basic breakfast of tea and toast and sat alone reading the proffered copy of that morning's *The Courier*.

There was no point in jumping straight in and making a fool of himself, he had not seen or heard of her since… he could not recall when exactly it was, not without a mental effort that he was beyond making just then. Had it been March or April of forty-three? He hoped *The Courier* would yield him its oracle's response. But he found he could not read it; the print wavered before his tired eyes and he crushed the broadsheet in his lap and leaned back in his uncomfortable chair.

'You alright?' a voice asked, and he looked up at the waitress, a dowdy woman who wore the war years as badly as did he.

'Fine, thanks,' he said, pulling himself together, just as he had so many times before when the alarms rang and he had found himself on the bridge without quite knowing how he got there or who had put his duffle coat and cap on.

He stepped out into the sunshine, determined to walk. Sailors do not walk much; up and down a bridge wing in time with the roll of their ship; up and down ladders, companion ways and gangways; a rushing, grasping progress from stanchion to lifeline along a corticene decking keen to fling him over a low bulwark; but not walking properly, not along country paths or city streets. He took off though, rolling slightly with a sailor's gait, staring up at the remnants of VE-Day bunting clinging to lamp-posts as he headed up the Grey's Inn Road and ultimately Fleet Street.

On the opposite side of the road he stood and looked up at Southmoore House, 'Home of *The Courier* and the *Evening Reporter*,' remembering it from all those years ago when he had come here for a job – an odd employment agency for a seaman. Beyond the mahogany doors with their polished brass furniture the lobby was the same, though older and dowdier from years of war and the dust of *Blitzkrieg*. The *belle époque* appearance seemed to mock now, rather than enunciate the power of imperial influence. Well, that was none of his affair; the country was on its knees and at least Southmoore House stood splendid among the ruins further along the road and up Ludgate Hill.

He hesitated a moment, eyed suspiciously by a uniformed commissionaire who wore medal ribbons from the Boer War. Just as the old man approached he made for the reception desk beside the lift-shaft. He had not prepared anything and simply said: 'I've come to see Elizabeth Southmoore,' in his most commanderly-like voice.

A frown crossed the receptionist's face. 'You mean Elizabeth Grant, the Late Lord Southmoore's daughter?' Her tone of voice was mildly incredulous.

Oh God, he thought, his heart now thumping at his effrontery, she is married. Well it was too late now. The tenacity with which he had pursued that last U-boat, seeking her in the beam of his frigate's sonar, losing her, then regaining contact to vector-in the little corvette *Daisy* and holding the echo to bring *Jonquil* in too so that the two of them sent their Hedgehogs and depth charges down to blow four score Germans into Hell, would not let him retreat. Married or not, he was here to see her and he had come a long way to do so. And at least he had run her to earth.

'Yes,' he replied smoothly.

'Is she expecting you, sir?'

'No,' he said, 'it's a surprise. I've, er, been away…in the navy.'

'What is your name sir?'

'Edward Adams, Commander Edward Adams if it makes any difference.'

The receptionist picked up her telephone and he turned away to watch the comings and goings of *The Courier*'s functionaries. It took a moment to register that the receptionist was trying to attract his attention.

'She's coming straight down, sir. Would you care to sit over there?'

'Thank you.'

She stepped out of the lift much as he remembered her on that last night at the Adelphi and his heart thumped. Then he realised she did not recognise him as she looked around the busy lobby. He stood up and she saw him.

'Edward,' she said coming towards him. 'I'm sorry, I didn't… the civilian clothes…but you're so *thin…*'

'Mrs Grant…' he held out his hand. No point in pretending that fragile intimacy of two-and-a-bit years ago remained. He would not stay, just make his number…

'What d'you mean…?' Her puzzlement changed to a laugh, taking his hand she drew him to her and turned back towards the lift. 'I'm not married; Grant was my family name. Besides, that last meeting…'

'When we drank to the end of the war?'

'Yes…'

They entered the lift, followed by a dishevelled young man who asked, 'd'you mind Miss Grant, only I've got something on the Lambeth murder.'

'Not at all, Gordon, hop in.'

They rode aloft in silence and it was not until they were in her office that they spoke again.

'You do look so dreadfully thin,' she said again, concerned, for there was something suddenly abject about him, vulnerable, all the hardness of their first encounter leached out of him.

He stood, his arms hanging down by his side. 'I am so very tired,' he replied in a piteous tone, swaying again as he had done outside the station.

'Sit down,' she indicated a chair by her desk. 'Would you like tea, or coffee, or something stronger?'

He shook his head. 'Nothing, thanks, I just wanted to see you…now that it's all over…'

Gone was the edgy half contempt of her former acquaintance. The man was so obviously shattered, on the verge of a nervous breakdown. 'You came specially to see me?'

'To London, yes. I don't really have anywhere else to go… my ship's in dry-dock and I don't know if I'm going back to her, she's slated for the Far East…'

She rang for coffee anyway and when it came he drank it and it seemed put new heart into him. She watched him pull himself together.

'I'm so sorry to dump myself on you like this,' he said, his voice stronger. 'I was near the end of my tether. It's the letting-go of the tension.'

He heaved himself up in the chair and stared about him. 'This was your father's office, if I remember correctly.'

She smiled. 'Yes, it was.'

'So are you *The Courier*'s editor?'

'No, I'm it's proprietor. I'll be ousted when all the men come home, but for now I'm the gaffer.'

He looked down at his coffee and then, seemingly suddenly emboldened asked: 'were you able to tell your father what happened to us on Kvitøya.'

'Yes, thanks to you, though I think he had guessed a good deal of it all.' She paused, then added, 'he died a few days later.'

'I'm sorry,' he said.

Now that he had directed their thoughts to the how-and-why of their acquaintanceship they both sat in silence, both thinking of that strange week in Liverpool and then they spoke simultaneously, and both spoke of the same thing.

'We said at the end of the war…' she said.

'I thought at the end of the war…' he said.

They broke off and smiled at one another. 'It was a kind of pledge, wasn't it?' he asked wearily and she could sense the anxiety in his voice.

'Yes, it was,' she replied, 'I had a plan to trace you…'

'Really?' his face brightened.

'Yes, really. You were a curmudgeonly fellow but I knew it was misanthropes like you who might actually win the war. And you did and we drank to the end of it and I have remembered you in my prayers ever since we said good-bye and you called me back after you remembered Bosun Tucker's name.'

It came out in a whoosh, so that he looked keenly at her. 'So I am not importuning you?'

She shook her head and he could see tears in her eyes. 'No, not as I once importuned you.'

'Yes, I was a bastard; I'm sorry. And you were buying me my dinner.'

'Oh,' she laughed, 'you were fine when I was buying you dinner.' She paused a moment and then asked, 'what are you doing for lunch?'

'Taking you out if you've the time and you'll come.'

'Of course I'll come. But where are you staying tonight?'

'I'm checked into a hotel near King's Cross.'

'That must be salubrious.'

'I've got three week's leave, then I shall call at the Admiralty and find out my future…'

'You'll stay with me tonight,' she said firmly and finally. 'I've a flat in Clarence Gate Gardens, off Baker Street. And tomorrow is Friday, we'll go down to my cottage in Essex, it's on the Stour. You can rest there for as long as you wish. It's very peaceful.'

'But I cannot…'

She got up and came towards him. 'Don't argue,' she said, bending and kissing him. 'Not now and not ever.'

Then she moved back to her desk, lifted the phone and began giving instructions that he did not listen to. Was this kindness real? Or some weird fantasy caused by his mental condition? When she looked up at him again she saw that he was quietly weeping.

'It's all over now.'

He nodded, and blew his nose. 'I'm sorry,' he spluttered.

'You have nothing to apologise for,' she said briskly, getting up and reaching for her coat as he wiped his nose. 'Now, you can buy me lunch.'

AUTHOR'S NOTE

Cold Truth is almost entirely a work of the imagination. The only fact in it is that in 1897, during the 'Heroic Age of Polar Exploration' an expedition was mounted by the Swedes. Its leader was Salomon Andrée who attempted to reach the North Pole by balloon (named *Eagle*, or *Örnen* in Swedish). This flight of the *Örnen* ended in disaster and its three occupants' end was on Kvitøya.

In 1999 I stood on the White Island of Kvitøya and first learned the tragic story of the 'Andrée expedition' from my Swedish shipmates. 'Andrée and his two companions are to us Swedes like Captain Scott and his men are to you British,' I was told, as they reverentially added stones to the lonely cairn raised in that bleak and unforgiving landscape. The story, with its sad and dark hints of morphine overdose, trichinosis and even cannibalism caught my imagination. Documentation exists to suggest at least the taking of morphine was suppressed, 'but kept a secret' and Danish analysis revealed trichinae present in polar bear meat shot by the adventurers. I have perhaps taken my greatest liberty with the notion of cannibalism. Hints of it persist, but it is odd that Andrée did not mention the death of Strindberg in his otherwise meticulous diary.

Such hints are – alas – grist to the novelist's mill. Thus embedded, they would not go away, but wormed their persistent way into the form of a story set, largely, aboard a type of vessel that had also captured my imagination when I had first gone aboard Scott's *Discovery* as a boy. The *Alert* is not so grand a barque as Scott's *Disco'*, but she is a tidy little craft which, once conjured up, had to go to sea somehow or other. As for her crew, I have met exemplars of all of them during a longish life, most of its spent at sea – which perhaps adds some few more 'facts' to my odd little tale.

April 2020.

Printed in Great Britain
by Amazon

65374612R00076